Survival of the Few

———◆o◆———

By Francis Edward Roberts

Eloquent Books

WIRRAL LIBRARY SERVICES	
500017786091	
Bertrams	23/05/2011
	£7.50
BI	

Copyright © 2010

All rights reserved – Francis Edward Roberts

No part of this book may be reproduced or transmitted in any form or by any means, graphic, electronic, or mechanical, including photocopying, recording, taping, or by any information storage retrieval system, without the permission, in writing, from the publisher.

Eloquent Books
An imprint of Strategic Book Group
P.O. Box 333
Durham, CT 06422

www.StrategicBookGroup.com

ISBN: 978-1-60911-864-8

Printed in the United States of America

Contents

Prologue	. . . .	v
Chapter 1	Life on the Hill	1
Chapter 2	A Strange Sound	13
Chapter 3	The Next Move	29
Chapter 4	The Killing Begins	39
Chapter 5	The Journey Begins	47
Chapter 6	Into the Forest	55
Chapter 7	The Group Splits Up	63
Chapter 8	Danger in the Forest	73
Chapter 9	A Strange Encounter	79
Chapter 10	Back Up North	83
Chapter 11	Two Go South	91
Chapter 12	Death of a Thousand Sheep	111
Chapter 13	Pyres by Night	119
Chapter 14	Phoenix and Hope	129
Epilogue	. . . .	141

Prologue

"Have I got a story to tell you," Father began, "a tale of faraway places, a tale of danger and courage in the face of great adversity!"

It seemed to be a day like many others before it. A cool, white mist rolled gently over the hills. It had the makings of a really good day. A bright spot in the sky toward the east showed that, when these first mists peeled away, there would be a warm sun shining down to cheer the hearts of all sheep on the Beacons. The Brecon Beacons that is, South Wales, where the grass is lush and the dangers are few, a most unlikely place for such a tale to begin.

"On this very hill is where our story begins, a few miles South of Brecon." He pointed to the north toward the little town where the Menflock live. "In fact, on this very hill lived your grandfather. His name was Tom. He and his partner Gwen were the parents of two very special lambs; twins they were. Well then, are you sitting comfy?"

"Yes, Father, I am ready," replied the little ram. He had bright, shining eyes, and little ears that never seemed to stop twitching, and such a wonderful smile. He had the broad shoulders of his father.

Father began to tell a tale that would prepare his little ram for the world around him, a tale of courage, bravery, and inner strength. "Okay then, here we go. Two long summers ago on this very same hill, things seemed very much as they do today. Your Grandmother Gwen was trying to get your Grandfather Tom to relax and enjoy their life together on the hill."

Chapter 1

Life on the Hill

GWEN took a deep breath. "Mmmmmmm, just breathe in that fresh air; isn't it wonderful to be back high on the hill? The first breath of spring, fresh grass all around, young ones jumping, and playing, feeding, and sleeping in the midday sun. Yes, it's the start of another wonderful summer in paradise."

"Yes, Gwen," said Tom in a convincingly uninterested manner. Well, after all, Tom had a very important job; he couldn't concern himself with such things. As Chief Ram, he stood around all day and looked out for danger; he had a flock to protect. He certainly looked the part; he was tall and held his head high at all times, except when he was eating grass of course. He had strong, broad shoulders and was always ready for action. Though, what that could possibly be he really couldn't imagine. After all, nothing bad had ever happened on Home Hill. Life was good.

"For goodness sake, Tom," said Gwen, "why don't you lighten up a bit! Enjoy the hills. When did anything ever happen up here to threaten us? We're hefted sheep and have pretty much looked after ourselves for hundreds of years. We're tough! We have to be; we spend half our time living in cold cloud mist. What other creature in its right mind would bother coming up here?" Tom looked a little disgruntled by her comments. He was convinced that, if he took a rest for just one minute, danger would come.

"Yes, Mother, you are right, we're tough, but keeping a good lookout is the very reason we have lasted so long with very little interference from the Menflock below." He was, of course, referring to the farmers in the lowlands. He was always curious about their lack of legs, not suited for the hill life at all really. "Anyway, enough of this chatter. I have work to do."

With a gentle sigh, Gwen whispered, "Yes, dear, I do love you, you stubborn old ram." She turned her face toward a strong shaft of warm sunlight, delighting in her lot in life.

A short distance away lazed her twin lambs, Hailwen, who was always up to something, and Bethan, who was a lot quieter than Hailwen but as clever as any little lamb and had a lovely smile. Well, they were sitting in the long grass, just staring into space. Their tails were wagging, their ears twitching, and they were contemplating, well, nothing at all really. They had full tummies, and fresh grass all around them, and not a care in the world. Mother watched them as they discussed whether or not to play a game until they finally decided to take some milk from mother. Gwen braced herself and waited for the inevitable butt in the stomach or ribs. "Here it comes." She closed her eyes as they descended upon here at a fair rate of speed. Bump! "One down, one to go." Crash! "Ow! Steady on, little one."

"Sorry, Mother," said Hailwen. "I tripped over that stone." Finally, they both settled down to a nice, warm drink of milk. Lambs' tails seem a little disjointed when they wag them hard. It's as though the end can't keep up with the speed of the beginning; it flails about all over the place, this way and that way with no control whatsoever. After a little while, they left off feeding from Mother. With tummies like drum skins, they once again to lay down flat in the long grass. They soon fell fast asleep.

Tom was still at his post watching over his family when he felt a presence at his side. It was Bo, short for Boyo, a little ram. Bo was adopted by Gwen and Tom a short while after their twins were born, but he was a little older than them and had all the makings of a fine, strong ram. There are a few different family breeds of Welsh Mountain sheep: There are white ones with long wool, like Tom and Gwen; speckled-face sheep; and black ones with shorter wool. Well, Bo was a Black Welsh Mountain sheep, an ancient breed, the toughest of all. They had been on these hills for thousands of years and had even grown some resistance to fly-strike and foot rot. Bo, as with all young ones, looked to Tom, his adoptive father, for guidance. "Hello, Father," he said in a low, shaky voice. "Do you mind if I help you?"

"If you wish, young one, but what can you do?"

The little ram thought for a moment, raised his little head as high as he could, and said, "Well, I am strong and growing very fast. I will soon have to duck to run under you." Tom looked a little disturbed at the prospect of the little ram not ducking at the crucial moment. "I would appreciate it if you also get the timing right," he said with his head tilted to one side, "if you know what I mean."

Bo thought for a moment and decided he didn't have a clue what Father was talking about, but trying to look as understanding as he could, he said, "Hmmm, yes, I see what you mean."

"If you want to help me, that's fine. One day you will stand here in my place, and you will need a lot of training." The little ram stretched his tiny, bony legs as much as he could and lifted his strong, solid little neck until his ears began to shake with the strain.

"Steady on, young one. If you want to do this job all day, you will have to learn to relax a bit."

Bo started shrinking, but only enough to stop his ears from shaking. He looked at Father out of the corner of his eye for some sign of approval.

"That's a bit better, little ram. Now let's get watching for danger."

Mother was standing a short distance away near the twins. She looked on as the Ramsfolk discussed the finer points of how to do absolutely nothing at all. She shook her head gently and turned to check on the twins, who were still lazing in the midday sun. All was fine on the hill, so mother began grazing to keep up her strength and to make sure there was plenty of milk for the twins.

"Mother," said little Hailwen.

"Yes, dear."

"My nose tickles. What's wrong with it?"

Mother strolled over to where the lamb was lying, looked at her little, shiny, wet nose, and said, "Oh, nothing to worry about, little one, it's only a thirsty fly taking a drink."

Hailwen screwed up her little face and said, "A drink! From my nose? That's disgusting!"

"Well," said Mother, "that's what it is, all right. You will get used to it soon; don't worry."

The little lamb was not convinced but tried to ignore the tickling fly. Mother, of course, knew that flies were a constant problem for sheep, and a full-blown fly-strike could kill the biggest ram. She was not sure if her little ones had the same inbred resistance to flies that their brother Bo might have. She had seen this happen a number of times on the mountain over the years and was sure to see it again, but she just hoped it wouldn't happen to one of them.

"Mother," Hailwen said again, "how many of us are there?"

Mother walked over to the little lamb and turned her toward the valley. "How many hills can you see?"

The lamb concentrated very hard and started counting, "One," and moved her head a little. "One," she said and moved her head a little more. She could count one because she was looking at it but had no concept of adding the number of hills together.

"Let me help a little," Mother interrupted, and she carefully pointed out all the hills in turn. "That's six hills, five valleys, and the low plain where the not-so-tough sheep live. Can you see the little white dots all over the hills?"

"Just about," said the lamb.

"Well, they are sheep like us."

Hailwen looked hard at the dots on the hill and said, "But, Mother, they are so tiny. I am much bigger than they are, and I am just a lamb."

The poor lamb had no concept of size or distance either. Mother smiled and continued, "When things are not close, they look small. When they are close, they look bigger."

The lamb turned to look at Father, who was some distance away, and said to Mother, "If that is the way of things, why does Father still look so big? He is all the way over there."

"It's best to just accept things as they are and not to worry about things you don't understand until you get bigger."

"Mother."

"Yes, Hailwen, what is it this time?"

"I have a headache."

"I am not at all surprised, all these questions! Look at your sister. She is just enjoying the sunshine."

The lamb looked over toward her sister, Bethan, and thought, "Hmmmm, maybe, but I think she is one blade of grass short of a full sod. One day, I will leave this hill and go to that hill over there." She looked into the distance. "Or that one."

Mother interrupted this moment of adventurous thinking and said, "Go, now, and rest your weary head, and you will feel better soon."

The little lamb went over to where her sister was lying and nestled in alongside her.

"Oh dear," Mother thought, *"poor little lamb, and so little patience. What will become of her?"* Mother watched them and smiled as they lay in the sun.

Meanwhile, Tom and Bo were still on guard duty doing what they were good at, absolutely nothing. Tom decided to graze a little so, after having a final check of the area, instructed Bo to remain vigilant at his post. The little ram was very proud to be given this promotion and stretched even higher to look the part as convincingly as Father did. Over the years, Tom had managed to balance the need to eat with the role of protector. He was still vigilant but wanted to give Bo the opportunity of feeling the responsibility for himself.

"Poor Bo," thought Mother, "he is trying so hard, standing there as straight as his little bones will let him."

With a bloodcurdling scream, the little ram dropped to the ground. "Help me! Help me! I've been captured," he screamed. The suddenness of the little ram's screams sent Tom into blind panic. He choked on his food and ran in circles trying to see what the threat was. What could be so awful to cause such terrible screams? Tom was so busy spinning around that he never even thought to ask Bo what the threat was or where it was coming from. Mother stood by watching this fiasco and looked at little Bo. She noticed that one of his back legs was sticking out straight as though pointing, but everyone knew that sheep only used their front legs to point, not their back ones.

"It's okay, everyone, don't worry, nothing to fear, don't worry."

Tom stopped spinning, and looked around, and then looked toward Mother. He looked a little angry at her comment. With his heart pounding in his chest, he tried to compose himself and was glad that all seemed okay. Mother walked over to Bo, by which time the rest of the family also stood over him.

"Ohh, it hurts," said Bo.

"Don't worry," said Mother. "I was afraid this would happen. You have been standing there far too long and don't yet know that the secret to doing absolutely nothing is to relax. You have cramp in your *bum*."

The whole family screamed with laughter at the plight of the poor little ram, more out of relief than anything else, but everyone was glad that no threat was approaching.

Tom felt a little uneasy about his reaction to this terrifying incident and so began trying to justify it by saying, "See, I told you I have to be alert all the time. Did you see the way I exploded into action and checked the perimeter? I told him to relax a little but, no, he had to scare the life out of all of you. It's a good job I was not scared," he said, peeping at Gwen out of the corner of his eye.

"Yes, dear," said Mother, "we all saw what you did and were very proud to have you looking over us." She was very careful not to embarrass Tom and was surprisingly successful at not bursting into laughter. Typical, though, of the female nature of any species, she was not going to let him off scot-free with his comments. Quietly whispering in his ear, she said, "Wipe your top lip, dear; you have beads of sweat all over it. But don't worry; your secret is safe with me."

She looked at him with a twinkle in her eye as he wiped the sweat from his lip. He grinned at his all-knowing partner, took a few deep breaths, and walked back to his post on the hill, a little shaken but no permanent harm done.

This episode played on his mind a little, and Tom couldn't help but wonder how indeed he would react in a real crisis; after all, this was the first time anything had ever happened. He hoped that the others couldn't see his bony legs still shaking as his knees passed one another shooting up and down like two kestrels looking for food in the grass.

After a while, all was calm again. Hailwen was sitting in the grass, her tail wagging again. She had either absorbed the lessons for the day or forgotten all about them. But it didn't really matter; all was good once more. Bethan was still enjoying the sun and had missed most of the commotion. She was dreaming of more hills, more valleys, and green, green grass. She just sort of let things happen and didn't seem fazed by anything at all. Tom was back in place with Bo at his side, his little butt cheeks still in and out of spasm from the cramps. Gwen was in the middle of it all, as usual, supporting Tom and proud of it.

Later that afternoon, Bo noticed a dark object moving along the bottom of the valley. "Pardon me, Father, may I speak?" he said respectfully.

"Yes, little ram, so long as you're not going to frighten the life out of everyone again. What is it?"

"Well," said Bo, "I just wondered, well, erm, noticed…" Bo was concerned about causing more trouble and was reluctant to say what was on his mind.

Tom turned to him and smiled. "Listen, my little ram, if you have a question, you ask it. That way, one day, you will know everything, like I do."

Bo looked up in awe at Tom and felt a little better.

Mother couldn't help overhearing what he said and strolled over to Tom. "Don't push your luck, big boy," she whispered in his ear.

Tom froze solid as he realised she had overheard his comment, and as she walked back to the twins, she heard him say, "Did I say *everything*? What I really meant was that you will know lots of things." Just a gentle reminder is all that was needed for Tom to keep his feet firmly on the ground. "Ask away, little ram," he said.

"I wondered what that is at the bottom of the hill, moving along in the valley."

Tom looked. His eyes were not what they used to be, but he knew what it was. He turned to Bo and said, "It's a fox."

Bo looked very worried, as his friends had heard stories of foxes coming into the flock and taking lambs to eat. "Are you going to fight with him?"

"Goodness, no, why would I want to do that?"

"Because he might kill us," exclaimed the little ram.

"Oh, I see," said Tom. "That old ewe's tale! You mark my words, little ram; that fox is a vixen, a *she* not a *he*. Her family have lived side by side with us on these hills for many generations, and we have never even had a cross word. You just watch and see what happens."

The fox, with a spring in her step, was walking along a well-used track, a path she had travelled many times before with sheep and lambs to her left and her right.

Tom asked, "Do you think, if those sheep felt threatened, they would move away from Mrs. Fox?"

"Yes, I suppose they would," Bo replied.

"Are they running away?" Tom asked.

"No, no, they're just looking," replied Bo.

"She is just walking right through the middle," Tom continued. "Remember well, little ram, not everyone you think may be an enemy will do you harm, but you were right to be cautious."

Tom had a good story to tell that might illustrate the point. "There was a sparrow sitting on a fence. It was a very, very cold day, so cold, in fact that the little bird froze to the spot. A large cow happened by and, after doing a big, erm, big poo, she swished her tail, knocking the poor little bird off the fence. Well, the little bird fell off the fence straight into the fresh pile of, erm, poo. Anyway, the, erm, poo was warm and squishy, and soon, the little bird started to thaw out, but he was still stuck in the, erm, the, erm, you know, the poo. Anyway, along came a cat and, after seeing the little bird, gently took hold of the bird and got him out of, of, the, erm, you know, the, erm, poo. When the little bird turned to the cat to thank him, the cat immediately ate him up in one big mouthful, and that was the end of that."

Bo was at a total loss to know why Father would tell him such a terrible story. Tom continued, "The moral of this tale is this: Just because someone drops you in the poo, that does not make him your enemy, and just because someone gets you out of the poo does not necessarily make him your friend."

Unfortunately for Tom, he had once again been overheard by Gwen. He saw her out of the corner of his eye. "Just telling it like it is, dear; that's all." Tom thought it best to retreat a little and backed away, mouthing a breathy whistle and showing a big, white top palate and a full set of bottom teeth as he went.

She came over to his side and whispered ever so gently in his ear. "If you ever, ever, tell that story to either of the twins ..." She paused. "Well ..." she paused again, "let's just say that you have to sleep sometime." She stepped back just enough to make eye contact. "It would be foolish on your part."

Tom felt a pang of sickness deep in his stomach. He, like all males, could only wonder about the possibility of unknown terrors that could be inflicted on him whilst he slept. He tried ever so hard not to gulp, but his Adam's apple felt like a rock in his throat. "Gulp," he whispered, "sorry, dear." And he gingerly walked back to his place to carry on watching.

Tom thought it best to get straight back to the conversation with Bo. "The Menflock who come up here at times always bring their dogs with them, but if you ever see a dog alone with no human to control it, then take care! Mostly it's lone dogs that kill our lambs, not foxes."

Bo gulped and carefully scanned the hillside for lone dogs just in case, but all was clear. He slowly relaxed a little. *So much responsibility, so much to learn,* he thought.

Tom knew that Bo was struggling with all of this so continued the lesson carefully. "The Menflock that come up here use dogs to gather us together, but neither their dogs nor these Menflock harm us; they just need our wool to keep warm, as most of them are as bald as a rock." They both grinned at this strange thought, then Tom continued, "The Manflock that comes to us has four dogs; three of these are used as sheep gatherers, but the fourth one is useless at it. He would rather come up here and talk to us, sit in the grass, and tell us stories about Menflock in the valley. They call him

Mad Dog because he is different from the others. He is a good friend of ours. Next time he is on the hill, I will introduce you to him."

"Oh yes, please, Father, that would be great," said Bo. He was learning so much today and he felt ever so grown up. It was a beautiful evening, the sun hung low in the sky, and it was as though it didn't want to go down at all. With vast areas of bright colours slowly stretching across the hills, a cool breeze carried the faint smell of mountain mist that brought the day to a gentle end. Yet another uneventful day on the hill. Well, almost uneventful!

Chapter 2
A Strange Sound

Bo woke with a start but was not too sure if someone had woken him up or if he had had a dream; in any case, the day seemed to start very abruptly. He looked around him to see that all was in its place, all his family accounted for. *Click!* A sharp noise caught his attention. *Click!* There it went again. "That's what woke me up; I wonder what it is?" He looked around but could see nothing. Tom was standing some distance away, so he made his way over to Mother. Mother was giving breakfast to the twins, and he didn't really want to disturb her, but *click!* The sound seemed to be getting closer, and he could stand it no longer, "Mother, I heard a strange sound!"

Click!

"You mean that one?" she asked.

"Yes. What is it?

"Well," she said, "I can tell you what it is, but I don't know how they do it."

Even more curious, he tilted his head to hear the strange sound once more.

Mother crouched down next to the little ram. "Look," she whispered, "can you see that large clump of grass sticking up just over there?" She pointed, with her front leg of course, in the direction of the noise. "Just watch it very, very carefully."

After what seemed like an age, *click!* The grass began to move. It rose slowly out of the ground. Bo got behind Mother. *Surely, that's not right,* he thought. Slowly, it rose even more to reveal the face of a Manflock all covered with mud, moving very slowly and looking all around.

"There you go; it's Menflock. There are more of them over there. They come here often."

Bo looked over to Tom to see if he was supposed to do anything about the strange goings-on or just observe. Tom must have known that the little ram was at a bit of a loss to know what to do, so he strolled over to where Mother and Bo stood. Mother smiled at Tom and made her way back to the twins to finish breakfast.

"Nothing to worry about," Tom said. "They are soldiers in the Manflock army. Mad Dog has told us all about them. They come up here to train and hide in the grass, to move around without being seen. That strange noise is something they use to talk to each other when they hide in the grass. They are very tough for Menflock, but they don't stay long. I think it's a bit cold for them."

"Hmmm," said Bo, "I understand, yes; bald as a rock, you said."

They smiled at one another then stood watching the soldiers for some time until a very loud whistle startled them all. A soldier at the bottom of the hill was calling to the others hidden in the grass. One by one, they stood up. There were more soldiers hiding than they had spotted. It was as though the ground were alive, but eventually, they all went down the hill and disappeared down the road in some very noisy, smelly trucks. "Now that is strange," said Tom. "They usually stay longer than that. I wonder what's wrong."

Mother walked over, leaving the twins to rest in the long grass. "What do you think, Tom?" she asked curiously.

"I don't know, but don't worry. I think I will have a word with Mad Dog and see if he knows anything."

"Okay and I will have a word with Vixen if she comes along later."

The usually calm atmosphere seemed to change to one of strange uncertainty. Tom said, "I think I will take a walk to the top of the hill to see if I can see anything. Ram-Bo, you are in charge of camp defence. Don't let me down now."

"No, sir, I mean, yes, sir. I mean I won't let you down." *Ram-Bo, he called me Ram-Bo, a Ram called Bo, Rambo. I like it; it sounds brave, warrior-like. Yes, I think I will keep it.* Rambo walked to higher ground and took up stag position. That's what they call the lookout. He stood bolt upright as proud as he could be but then relaxed just a little bit, remembering the cramp-in-the-bum incident. *I'll show them I can do a good job,* he thought, and there he stood, feeling as tall as Tom, his father.

Tom made his way to the top of the hill and looked around. He could see Brecon, where the Menflock lived, to the north. He could see lots of sheep on the hills, and everything looked as it should. As he scanned the valley below, he saw a small red square at the bottom of the next valley and then another one farther along. The second red patch was a lot bigger than the first and was about halfway up the next hill. He had no idea what these objects could possibly be; there had never been anything like them on the hills before. Tom was not willing to dismiss them without further investigation. He looked back down the hill to his family and, as all was safe and he could see no danger on the hill, he decided to go and investigate the strange events. It took quite a long time to get down the hillside, but eventually, he arrived at the position of the smaller red patch. As he ventured more closely, he was startled by a sound. "Pssst."

He turned but could see nothing. He walked forward once more until suddenly a crazed dog ran straight at him, barking, snarling, and teeth flashing like knives. Tom just shut his eyes and waited for the inevitable to happen, but nothing did! After a second or two, he slightly opened one eye to see Mad Dog standing before him.

He breathed a sigh of relief to see his friend and was just about to say something when Mad Dog vanished. He looked around once more. "What is going on? Have you actually gone crazy? Where are you, Mad Dog? What is the matter?"

"I'm over here." He followed the direction of the sound to find his friend in the bottom of a drainage ditch. "Get down here quick," Mad Dog said desperately.

"But …"

"No buts, just get down here now, please, Tom, please."

Tom got down into the ditch with Mad Dog. "You're not going to eat me, are you?"

"No, I've already eaten."

Tom was not exactly comforted by this remark.

"I was joking," Mad Dog said, and Tom breathed out once more.

"I knew that; I did. I knew that."

"Hmmm, okay, if you say so. Tom, you have to listen to me. I am not supposed to be here. They have locked up all the other dogs. I escaped to find you. Some Menflock came to the farm today from the ministry."

"What's that?" asked Tom.

"Just listen. I don't quite know what's going on yet, but I do know the farmer was very upset. He was told to lock up all the dogs, and they have killed his best bull and all his cows. They are coming up here next."

Tom looked over at the red object and could now see it was filled with holding pens. He had seen these many times before but not covered over as this one was.

Mad Dog continued, "They are looking for a disease called the foot and mouth, and they think you all might have it."

"That's ridiculous," said Tom. "What is this disease? Does it kill sheep?"

"No, I think it gives you sore feet," replied Mad Dog.

"Sore feet!" exclaimed Tom. "I have never met a sheep that didn't have sore feet, especially when the Menflock see you limping. They catch hold of you and cut half your hoof away. I'll tell you about sore feet."

"*Stop!*" Mad Dog interrupted. "You must listen to me. If they come here and find the disease, they will kill you and your family as sure as they have just killed the cows. They will kill you all."

Silence fell over the two friends as they absorbed the terrible possibilities of these events. A sudden realisation of the situation hit Tom. He spun around and looked at the hill on which he had left his family, and immense guilt swept over him. "Oh, no, I have left Gwen and the others on the hill. I am not there to protect them. What have I done? What have I done?" Tom began to scramble up the bank out of the ditch, desperate to get home, but Mad Dog grabbed his leg and dragged him back into the muddy water. "I have to go," Tom cried desperately. "I have to get back. Please, Mad Dog, please let go of my leg. Please help me."

Mad Dog tried to calm his friend. "I will help; that's why I am here. I escaped to find you, and I am not going back, but we need to be very careful. If I am spotted, I will be shot, and if you are spotted, you will never get back to your family."

A strange noise was wafting on the air, buzzing like flies, and then it was gone. No, wait! There it was again. "What is that noise?" asked Tom.

Mad Dog looked worried.

"What is it?" he said again.

"Quads," replied Mad Dog. "Sometimes the farmer gives us a ride up the hill on the back when we're working." The noise was coming from the direction of home, and Tom was getting very agitated. "Tom, Tom, you have to listen to me. We will get there if you do as I say." Mad Dog explained how they would be able to get back onto the hill by staying low. Using the drainage ditches and natural gullies on the hillside as cover, they could make their way slowly up to the top of the hill. From there, they could see what was going on.

"Okay,' said Tom, "but let's go now before it's too late."

It was getting late, and it had been a many hours since Tom left little Bo on guard. *What a terrible responsibility for one so young,* Tom thought, as they set out up the hill. They were about halfway home when it went dark. Desperate to carry on, they continued for a while until they both fell exhausted behind a crumbling wall for a rest. Tom was very restless but tried to get some sleep. He remembered the soldiers hiding in the grass and thought how glad he was that he had watched them move through the terrain without being spotted. He hoped he had learned enough to get home. "Oh, why did I have to have a white coat? Who in their right mind would wear white? I can be seen for miles," he mumbled to himself.

Just before first light, they planned their route home. They had an advantage today. The mist hung low on the hills, so the Menflock would find it hard to see them covertly sneaking up the hill like Menflock soldiers. They stopped occasionally to listen, but this only made Tom more anxious. He could hear quad bike engines roaring. The sound seemed to be coming from all over the place. In the mist, the sound was just whirling in the air. They could now also hear the faint sounds of sheep bleating as they were forced down the hill. It was just after midday when they reached the top of the hill. The mist began to clear. Soon, they would be able to see what was going on.

As the mist cleared, they could only see one white dot. All of the other sheep had gone. Tom felt sick with anxiety, but as they looked toward the bottom of the hill, they noticed yet another red patch that was not there when he left the hill yesterday, and they could hear many sheep penned up inside it. They could only hope that the others were in that pen but wondered how to get to them.

Mad Dog moved over to Tom and, in a low, determined voice, said, "Don't worry, my friend, we're not beaten yet."

The single white dot on the hill didn't seem to move much, and once again using the cover of a drainage ditch, they set off toward it. When they got there, it turned out to be one of Tom's oldest friends; they used to play together as lambs. Keeping low, they moved closer to see what was going on. The old ram was lying in a hollow in the ground; his leg was badly broken, and a large piece of gleaming white bone was sticking out. "Oh, Tom, it's good to see you, my old friend."

Tom was speechless. Just how was he to help his friend?

His injured friend continued to speak, "Listen carefully. You two can't stay here; the Menflock are coming back up the hill to finish me off. I fell, you see, boyo. They ran into me with their quad when they were rounding us up, and they have gone to get a vet to kill me. They will be back soon. You must not get caught."

He sounded so weak and looked very frightened. Tom turned to Mad Dog, "What are we to do? We can't just leave him here."

Mad Dog looked at him but he knew that they could do nothing to help.

"You must leave, both of you, *now! Please!* Look, they are coming back up the hill." Sure enough, the Menflock were coming up the hill toward the old ram.

"I can't do this. I can't leave you, my friend."

"You have no choice, Tom, but you can do one last thing for me."

"Anything! What do you want us to do?" replied Tom, desperately seeking a solution.

"My partner, Slight, was visiting your Gwen. She was taken below with your family. Please get her out and take care of her; she is very fragile."

"Yes, of course I will."

Mad Dog was getting a little anxious. "We have to get away from here, quickly. Quickly! The ditch!"

They turned and ran back to the cover of the drainage ditch, and both dived headlong into the mud. They lifted their brown, muddy faces from the earth, and Tom sneezed. Two plugs of brown, wet mud shot out of his nose. They looked on while the two Menflock made preparations to kill his friend. With a sharp stab, they forced a poison into his neck. He looked over to where Tom and Mad Dog were hiding. Tom felt a terrible pain in his heart as though he himself had been stabbed with the lethal concoction. After a few minutes, his friend gently nodded his head this way, then that way, and finally, he was dead. A terrible numbness engulfed them. "Goodbye, my old friend, I will miss you." He turned to Mad Dog and said, "What is to become of us? What are we to do?

Mad Dog could see that his friend needed his support. "It will be dark soon, and all the Menflock will be going home for the night. As soon as they go, we will go down to the pen and rescue the others."

Finally, darkness fell and the one-dog, one-ram rescue team was ready. The Menflock had gone to their homes for the night, so it was time to go down to the pen that held the rest of the family. As they approached the pen, they realised the task was not going to be easy.

"It's so big," said Tom. "How will we ever find them? There must be thousands of sheep in there." As they considered the options, Tom finally asked, "Can you click your fingers?"

Mad Dog looked at him. He looked at his feet and then back at Tom. "Tom, I'm a dog. I don't have fingers."

"Oh, okay, just a thought."

"Why did you ask that?" Mad Dog asked.

Tom explained how he had had a conversation with Bo the previous day about how the soldiers talked to each other in the grass by making a clicking sound. "If we could make that sound, little Bo just might hear it and come over to us at the side of the pen. That just might work, if only we could make that noise."

"Well, let's not give up yet. I might have been useless as a sheepdog, or so they said, but I have spent a lot of time with the Menflock. I can try to make the noise with my tongue."

Oh dear, thought Tom, *he's lost it. He has actually gone mad.*

"Just let me try," said Mad Dog.

Never argue with a sick mind, thought Tom, as he attempted a nervous smile.

Mad Dog tried, and tried, and tried, and suddenly, "Click."

Tom was visibly shocked. "Do it again; do it again," said Tom excitedly.

"Click, click, click, click, click, click."

"Fantastic!" cried Tom. "Let's do it."

They carefully made their way down to the pen, keeping a careful watch just in case the Menflock left someone to guard their captives. All was clear. As they approached the pen, Mad Dog licked his lips a couple of times, pulled some very strange faces, and, "Click." A few seconds later, "Click, click," and again, "click, click."

An old ewe turned toward them. "Just what the hell are you pretending to be dog? Are you mad?"

"I have my moments," said Mad Dog. "We're trying to find a little ram named Bo. We thought—"

"Well, don't think," said the old ewe. "You will hurt your head."

Mad Dog was so angry that he almost felt a growl coming on. His upper right lip quivered, and ever so briefly, a sharp, white canine tooth flashed in the dark.

"Don't you show those teeth at me! I'll come over there and slap you purple," said the old ewe. She turned to her daughter standing alongside and said, "Go over to the far side of the pen. I saw them over by the stream. Tell Gwen that Tom is here."

The ewe's daughter squeezed and jostled this way and that way. "Excuse me, oops, sorry." It was tough going, but she never gave up.

She was missing for quite a while, but eventually, she returned and said to Tom, "I found them, but they will never get through the flock; we're too tightly packed. I have told them to stay exactly where they are, and you will come to them."

"Oh, thank you, thank you so much. Where are they?"

"Go to the lowest part of the pen near the stream by a large boulder and call her."

Without hesitation, they followed the fence line down the hill. When they reached the boulder, they called again and again, and just couldn't get a reply. Mad Dog licked his lips once more.

Tom smiled. "Go for it, Mad Dog; do your stuff."

"Click, click." He was getting quite good at this. "Click, click."

A few minutes later, Bo burst through a wall of wool headlong into a fence post. "Uugh, over here, we're all over here."

"Oh, Bo," cried Tom, "are you all okay?"

"Yes, I kept us all together. Stay here; I will bring them to you."

He vanished once more, and shortly afterward, they were all reunited. Face to face once more, Tom and Gwen exchanged looks of relief and worry in the same instant.

"Bo," said Tom.

"Yes, Father," he replied.

"You have done an excellent job. Thank you."

The little ram felt very proud.

"What's going on, Tom?" Mother asked.

"No time for that now. I'll tell you later. Right now, we have to get you all out of here."

While they were talking, Mad Dog had already been working on the escape plan. He was biting his way through the orange bailing twine holding the gate closed. "There, that's it."

The gate swung open, and Mother, the twins, and Bo were free.

"What's Mad Dog doing here?" asked Mother.

"No time now, talk later," said Tom. "Stay together, and follow us up the hill, but first, do you know where Slight is?"

"Yes, she came down with us. Why?"

Tom didn't answer her. Now was not the time to tell her of the plight of this old friend. "Bo, will you go and get Slight?"

"Yes, sir."

When they returned, the whole group began their journey and made their way up the hill. Mad Dog stopped. "Tom, you take your family to the muddy pool at the top of the hill. I will meet you there."

"Where are you going?" asked Tom.

"I have to tell the old ewe what is going on, so they too have a chance to escape."

"Okay, see you up there."

"Escape?" said Gwen. "What did he mean? Escape what?"

Taking care not to let the others hear, Tom explained to Mother what was happening. The story definitely put an extra spring in her step as they retreated to the top of the hill.

Mad Dog approached the old ewe.

"I had hoped we haaad seen the last of you. What is it now?"

Mad Dog explained why they had rescued the others and how the Menflock were going to kill them all. To his surprise, she said, "If you had brains, you would be dangerous. You come here clicking like no animal I've ever heard and expect me to believe such rubbish. The Menflock need our wool; that's all. They won't kill us."

Mad Dog was so frustrated, but the stubborn old ewe just would not listen to his pleading. "The gate is open in case you come to your senses. Good luck." Mad Dog vanished into the darkness once more to meet up with his friends at the top of the hill.

The others arrived at the mud pool around midnight. Tom explained to Gwen that they must all be covered in mud to hide their white coats. Mother was not impressed, yet one by one, they were all immersed in the mud, yes, including Mother.

"We all need to rest," said mother. "It's very late, and the young ones are tired."

"Yes, rest now. I will look out for Mad Dog." Tom explained to Mother that the only way to survive this situation was to evade capture and make like the soldiers hiding in the long grass that they had so often watched with curiosity.

Mad Dog had found a bag of sandwiches left behind by the Menflock. He carried them to the top of the hill with him. "I suggest we all eat something. It won't be easy to move in daylight," said Mad Dog. The sandwiches went down a treat, and the sheep grazed, pretending it was all a bad dream.

"Oh, Tom, what is to become of us?" Mother whispered.

"You just stay close and look after the twins. We will be fine." She couldn't see that Tom had his back legs crossed as he said it, but truth be told, he just didn't know what was going to happen. Mother and Slight tended to the twins while Mad Dog, Tom, and little Bo whispered deep into the night to decide the best form of action to take in the morning. It was a cold night, as spring had not yet fully lifted its friendly face, and a clear sky made it all the more necessary to huddle the rest of the family into a corner of their small retreat in a hollow in the ground at the top of the hill.

The following day started with an eerie silence; Mother was the first to waken. It seemed so strange to look over the hill and not see any other sheep out grazing. And then came the realisation that this was no dream; this was really happening. The mist lay heavily on the top of the hill like fine wool, but from their little hide, it was hard to see the bottom of the hill where so many of their friends were held captive in the big pen. Mother looked at Tom and thought it best to wake him first so that he could prepare himself for the question that would inevitably come. "What are we to do, Daddy?" Yes, that was the one; they all wanted to know the answer to that one. A plan had been worked out, but now was not the time to discuss it.

"Shhhhh!" whispered Mad Dog. "Get down. Tom, come over here." The dog was crouching very close to the ground as only a sheepdog can; even his ears seemed to be touching the floor.

Tom walked over and dropped on his front legs to his knees, but his bottom was still swaying in the air as only a sheep's can.

"Look," said Mad Dog. "White dots. Maybe you are not the only ones not yet captured by the Menflock."

Tom looked down the hill. The mist had begun to clear, and yes, he too could see about a dozen or so white dots outside the pen at the bottom of the hillside. He turned to the group, "Bo, come over here for a moment; you've got better eyes than me. Can you see those sheep?"

Bo squinted his eyes, twitched his little nose, and after a moment, his eyes widened, and his head went forward. "Yes, I can see all right." The whole group seemed to be uplifted by the thought of others on the loose like themselves. "Let me finish." Bo was very abrupt, and the whole group fell silent. "I can see them, but they are not sheep." They looked at one another.

"Just what can you see then? What are the white dots?" asked Tom.

"Menflock, I can see Menflock in white skins, lots of them, and they are going into the big pen where all the sheep are held."

A sickening fear spread through the group. Mad Dog looked at Tom, and they nodded toward each other, remembering that men in white skins killed Tom's friend with the broken leg, Slight's partner. They had not yet told her of his plight. Mother was allowing the twins to feed, thinking that, if they were feeding, they would not be worried by the tension amongst the adults. The little lambs may have been feeding, but Bethan, who seldom said a word, pulled away from her mother. Her little tail actually stopped wagging for a moment, and she said, smacking her lips with her tongue with a white ring of milk around her mouth, "If you ask me, that's a good thing."

"What is?" asked Mother. The rest of the adults looked at Bethan.

"Well," she continued, "if all the sheep are gone from the hillside and all the Menflock are wearing white skins, we will be able to see them coming." On finishing her sentence, she immediately nuzzled into her mother's teat for more breakfast.

The group was totally silent, stunned by the validity of this comment, and from such a little one. Slowly, Tom turned his head toward Bethan, his mouth hanging open in amazement. He turned to Mother. Mother gestured to him to close his mouth, and he, realising how silly he must look, closed it quickly. "What did she say then?" Tom asked, looking at Mother.

"Oh! Out of the mouths of babes," she said, "out of the mouths of babes. She said, my dear, if the Menflock are all wearing white, we will be able to see them coming."

The whole group turned to the little lamb, but she was far too busy for their praise; she was having breakfast. Mad Dog started to laugh. "Isn't this a turnabout? Only a few days ago, the sheep were white, and the soldiers were covered in mud. Now, the Menflock are all white and the sheep are covered in mud."

This was the light-hearted moment that they all needed. Tom, as usual, took everything a stage further, "You're right; little one was right. But if we have changed sides, let's take advantage of it. Some of those soldiers were special soldiers; we're special sheep. We arn't lowland sheep; we're a hefted flock and much tougher than most other sheep. We're the Welsh Mountain Special Flock, the W.M.S.F."

Oh, good grief, thought Mother, *what next?* She grinned as usual, but inside, she did wonder whether Tom was under just too much stress. *Boys will be boys,* she thought. "Sounds a bit of a mouthful," said Mother.

"As it may be," replied Tom, "but if we're to get through this, we better start thinking like soldiers."

Mad Dog coughed quietly then said, "Excuse me, I don't want to dampen this in any way, but in case you haven't noticed, I am a dog, not a sheep."

Tom turned to Mad Dog, saying, "No matter, the W.M.S., erm, F. would not be here if not for you, so we're going to call you Shadow. Yes, Shadow."

"Why Shadow?" asked Mad Dog, looking a little confused.

"Because you are fast and disappear into thin air."

"Hmmm, I do, don't I? Wow, a proper name," said Shadow. "I've never had one of those before."

Tom continued, "Well, that's it then. The W.M.S.F. is now an active unit."

Mother was looking on patiently until she could hold back no longer. "I'm so glad we sorted that out, but have you decided what we're to do?"

"Excuse me," said Bo. "I also have decided on a new name. I wish to be called Rambo."

The group turned to the little ram. Tom thought for a moment, looked at the rest of the group, and said, "Well, I think that's a very good name, and you have earned it. Rambo it is."

Rambo looked ever so proud.

"Now," said Tom, "we have to discuss our next move, but first I have to talk to Slight." Tom took her to one side and told her that her partner had been killed by the Menflock. The group fell silent.

Chapter 3
The Next Move

RAMBO was on guard duty or stag, as it was otherwise known. He was the only one with eyes good enough to see what was going on below at the pen. It had been decided that Shadow was to be the recon unit, to go ahead and bring back information needed to move the group. He was the fastest and fittest, a good fighter, good at concealment and at evading capture, and he knew more about the Menflock than the others did, so it was a natural role for him to play. Rambo, because he had proven his worth, was also assigned to bring up the rear while the group was mobile to watch for danger from that quarter.

"Where do I fit into all this bravado?" Mother asked.

"Gwen, you, my dear, are the mother of my little lambs, my reason to live. You tend the little ones with Slight at your side to help when we need to move."

Tom was not known to make romantic speeches such as this, and Gwen's heart just swelled up with love for the big dope. The whole group now had a role to play. Now they needed to know what Shadow, Tom, and Rambo had decided the previous night.

All were well camouflaged with mud and blended in very well against the surrounding hillside. It had been decided that, so long as it was deemed safe to stay put in the little dip at the top of the hill, they would stay there for one more day at least to see whether the sheep below were released from the big pen.

The day's silence was occasionally broken by distant sounds of sheep bleating. The sound was carried on the light breeze moving over the hills. The mist lifted about midday, and for a while at least, the sun made them feel a little better about their plight. Slight and Gwen talked of her life with her partner and other motherly things and worked together to occupy the twins, not a task that was envied by the males of the group. If it were down to them to carry out this role, they would probably run down the hill and give themselves up, but helping Gwen with the twins was just what Slight needed at this time.

During the afternoon, quads patrolled the hillside on two occasions but didn't spot this little band of refugees. Rambo kept watch on the goings-on below, as assigned, and as far as he could tell from such a distance, the sheep were still moving around inside the pen. The Menflock were moving amongst them, but he couldn't make out exactly what they were doing. Eventually, the men below left the hillside mostly in the direction of Brecon, just a few miles north of them.

Shadow said, "In a little while, I will go down to the pen and talk to the sheep. They may be able to tell us what the men have been saying and what their plans are."

"Okay," said Tom, "that's a good idea. When you get back, we will see if we need to carry out our plan. Firstly, though, let's go over our plans again for later on." Tom, Shadow, and Rambo sat in a huddle to discuss their plans once more.

They were camped at Bwich Duwynt (grid ref 005 210). Tom had found a discarded map of the hills some time before and, being the cautious ram that he was, kept it safe for just such an eventuality. "You should never confuse paranoia with being prepared," his great grandfather used to say. He remembered his great grandfather sitting him on his knobbly knees when he was very small and telling him of a similar incident happening in Wales up in the north somewhere many years before. It just so happened that this map might be very useful. They were aware that, although they had been safe so far in their little hiding place, they would need the cover of woodland if they were to remain free. The map showed a small area of woodland below them, but it was a bit too close to the pen for comfort. They had decided to go southeast to reach Taf Fechan Forest. It was huge; they could hold out in there for ages, and anyway, this might be all over by tomorrow.

"Now," said Tom, "we have two options from here. We can drop down the valley to our east, down to Tor Y Bigwns, and follow the Blaen Taf Fechan down to the Upper Neuadd Reservoir, and follow the west bank past the dam, Neuadd House, and on to the Taf Fechan Forest. On the other hand, we can stay on the top of the hill, and follow the ridge along Craig Gwaun Taf down to Craig Fan Ddu and along until we see the pile of stones, and turn east there into the forest. What do you think, Shadow?"

"Well, if we drop to the east and follow the river, we might have more cover, but we would have to cross about twenty small streams feeding into the Blaen Taf Fechan. That may be very difficult, especially with the twins."

"What do you think, Rambo?"

Rambo's blood ran cold. He had never been asked an important question before. "Hmm, hmm." He cleared his throat. "Well, I think we should stay on the top of the hill. According to this map, we would have to drop about a hundred meters to reach the river. That would be hard even before we reach the little streams."

And didn't he do well! Tom looked at them both. "Well, that's decided then. We stay on the ridge, but I do suggest we drop just a few metres from the track, so our shapes don't stand out against the sky behind us."

All agreed, and the plan was set in stone, well, in mud anyway.

Still, with a couple of hours of daylight left, Shadow said, "The men have gone now, so I am going to check the ridge for later."

"Are you sure you won't be too tired?" asked Rambo.

"What, me? No. I'm a sheepdog, Mad Dog by name, mad dog by nature." He definitely was not designed to sit still for such an extended period. Shadow sprung to his feet and, taking hold of a muddy stick, wrote "Born to Run" on his last remaining white patch. Then he was gone, bolting off into the distance, singing, "Who let the dogs out, woof , woof, woof, woof, woof," and vanished.

Mother turned to Tom, "What was on those sandwiches he ate?"

Tom replied, "I don't know, dear, but I wish I had some."

The words "who let the dogs out" gently faded into the distance as Shadow went along the track. Rambo watched the pen below, but it didn't seem as lively as it was before the Menflock went into the pen, but at least the sheep were still moving about. Rambo was scanning the hillside, watching for quads or for anything that might be important, when he saw a lone white dot coming along the ridge toward their position. "Father," he whispered, "look over there." He pointed north toward Corn Du. "That track leads directly to us. What shall we do?"

Tom looked over, but whatever it was, it was too far for him to tell. "Give it a few minutes. Let me know when you can see what it is."

Rambo looked at the figure as it moved slowly toward them. "It's a sheep, Father. It's one of us."

Tom looked excitedly. "We stay hidden. If that track does come straight to us, and he or she is not spotted, then we will call them in."

"Come on," whispered Rambo, "keep going."

They all wished the new arrival along, hoping that they would get to the hide. "Oh, no," said Tom, "that noise again. It can't be;

it can't be a quad. I thought they all went home." But it was indeed a quad. A couple of the Menflock had stayed behind to patrol the hill for strays to round up. Tom turned to the group, "Get down everyone, right down, and don't make a sound." The quads roared up the hillside toward the unfortunate, lone sheep that was still coming toward them. "Stop, stop, you stupid animal. Go away; you must go away," Tom said through gritted teeth and palate. "Turn away." The sheep was no more than about a hundred metres away when it spotted the quads and stopped to look. It was as though the animal were in shock; it just stood there looking. The quads roared toward it and then pushed the animal off the track and down the hillside toward the big pen at the bottom of the hill. "Keep still, everyone; keep very still," warned Tom as one of the riders stood up high on his machine to scan the horizon. It seemed a very long time. For a few seconds, he looked directly at the dip where they were hiding, and then sat down, and revved his engine. The quad was coming for them. "Don't move; just wait. If he has seen us, there is no use running. We're better staying together," said Tom.

The quad was only about fifty metres away when it suddenly turned west and began to go down the hill toward the pen below. The whole group let out a heaving sigh and closed their eyes for a few seconds. "Gosh, that was so close," said Slight, turning to Mother.

"Too close for my shattered nerves," she replied.

Tom turned toward the little band of worried sheep. "The sooner we make a move, the better. If Shadow is not back by dark, we're going. Hopefully, we will meet him on the track."

While Tom and the rest of the group were having a most anxious time, Shadow was having adventures of his own. On arrival at the forest, he passed a pile of stones on his right. He remembered that they discussed this pile of stones shown on the map as the point that they would use to enter the forest. He was at the uppermost northwest corner of the forest, and as he approached, he noticed a track directly ahead of him. "It will be time to head back soon, but I will just have a little look inside while I am here." It was dusk, and the sun was setting behind him. The rays of the sun penetrated deep into the woodland. It seemed to go on and on and on, as far as the eye could see. As he strolled along the path, everything was so peaceful, unlike the top of the hills, where the wind never seemed to stop. He almost forgot what all the fuss was about.

"*Aaaaahhh!*"

"What was that?" He squatted as low as he could and slithered to the side of the track. "Ha, ha, ha, ha, ha, you silly beggar." Menflock! There were Menflock in the forest. He stayed as low as he could and moved forward. As he crept forward, he was very briefly confronted by a man who was tumbling down a steep hill. He was grabbing at trees as he went, this way, that way. He hit a number of trees really hard then, finally, "Gotcha," he said as he caught hold of a small tree and stopped sliding. His mate was still laughing at the poor man's plight.

Shadow watched for a moment, his head turned at an angle to view this unfortunate event from the victim's perspective, then whoosh, he was off again. A tree that had been dislodged at the top of the hill followed him down. It hit the man across his back and sent him sliding once again. Well, this was just too much excitement for the man at the bottom, who was taking a drink of water from his can. After spurting like a fountain, he was on his knees laughing at his mate, who didn't look as though he was enjoying this ride one little bit. Once again, he managed to catch a tree and stop his decent. Shadow was sitting in a bush watching the whole thing unfold, but it was not yet over. The sliding tree, which seemed to be armed with some sort of tracking device, hit the man again.

Oops, I bet that hurt, thought Shadow, and the strange saga continued. He was on the move yet again. He must have wondered if this hill was ever going to end. Suddenly, he burst through the undergrowth and, after a short drop, landed on the track right at the feet of his mate.

"No badgers up there," he said.

Shadow's blood ran cold. He thought about this comment for a moment. "No badgers up there. That's it! I thought I recognised them. These men are from the ministry. They're Badger Boys. They used to visit the farm back home to survey, trap, and kill badgers for the government, some disease control trial, I think." He was worried that these men too would be called in to track and kill. After all, that's what they did for a living. It would be almost impossible to escape these Badger Boys.

"I don't know about you, but I've had enough for one day. I feel like I just fell down a mountain."

His mate was still laughing. "Ya just did. It was amazing. Tee-hee-hee, I've got a bellyache."

"Oh, right. Anyway, thanks for your help back there."

"You're welcome," he replied as he fell forward, once more prone to spasms of laughter. "Batman. Da, da, da, da, da, Batman." He spread his arms, pretending to fly.

"Idiot, I'm gonna get a new partner," he said to his laughing friend.

"Oh yeah, and where do you think you will get anyone to look after you like I do?"

This banter continued as they gradually disappeared at the bottom of the track until Shadow could hear the laughter no longer. After a quick look around the area, he decided he would get back to the others on the hill. He ran back along the track and in the direction of his friends on the hill. As he ran, his thoughts returned to his home, to sitting in front of the range. It was huge; it had about six ovens and a big old grate in the middle. Thinking about it, he could never remember that fire ever being allowed to go out. It was a cold evening, and the thought of this fire at home seemed to warm him, or it could have been that he was running as fast as his legs would carry him. Anyway, he recalled sitting by the fire listening to the farmer talking to the Badger Boys while they drank tea and ate large pieces of homemade fruitcake sitting around the big old table. It was a big square one that made him jump every time the Mrs. would pull out the extension bits. *Bang* it went as it dropped into place. *Always made me jump, that old table,* he thought. It had those twisty legs and big knobbly feet. *I had my own rug,* he remembered. *I wonder what has happened to the cat,* he thought. She used to sleep all day long curled up in the bottom oven of the range. *Gosh, it must have been hot in there.* It was dark now, and the track seemed to go on and on. He recalled some of the conversations that the farmer had had with the Badger Boys. "Well then," the farmer said, "you tell me what you found, and I tell you if you're any good at trackin', 'cos I know this 'ere piece of earth like the back of my hand." The Badger Boys looked at one another and smiled. They knew their job all right. They pointed out every badger set, fox earth, and rabbit warren on the place, even some spots where all three seemed to live together. "Well, I'll be," said the farmer, "not bad, you aren't, not bad at all." After this, the farmer seemed to warm to them; they had shown him they were definitely not the normal ministry types. *Yep,* the farmer thought, *a couple of good uns.* Shadow knew it would only be a matter of time before the Badger Boys were called in.

In fact, unknown to him, they already had been called in and had been dispersed across the countryside to trap wildlife on and around infected farms. The countryside was a very unsafe place for all animals, but especially for him and his friends. Shadow ran and ran. *Soon be there now, soon be there now. At least,* he thought, *these Badger Boys could be easily spotted.* They drove around in great big, green Land Rovers, so if he looked out for their vehicles, he would know they were nearby.

He was just a few hundred metres away from the dip in the ground where he left his friends. It seemed such a long time ago now. He stopped, listened, and looked at the dip. No movement.

His heart felt like a lead weight. "Oh no, please be there, please be there." He edged his way along slowly, not wanting to move at all. Still he could see nothing. Just a few meters to go, ever closer, until he could finally see into the hollow. It was empty! He rested on his belly; his legs felt too weak with fear for his friends. Feeling desperately alone, he whimpered.

"Psst. Hey, Shadow, what you doin' over there?"

His heart nearly burst with fright and excitement all rolled into one. He was looking into the wrong hole. In one giant leap, he landed right in the middle of them. "Oh, thank goodness, this is great; I thought you were all gone."

"No, we're all here," said Tom.

Shadow told them he had checked the track right to the forest and even looked into the forest. He thought it best not to tell them about the Badger Boys in case they would not go. He didn't know they had already had one close call on the hill and that nothing would convince them to stay. "You had a good day then?" said Shadow, still trying to slow his heart rate.

"Oh, fine," said Tom, not wanting to worry him about leaving them again.

"Ok, that's fine then," said Shadow, curling up next to the twins. "Any news from below?"

"No, but Rambo is going down there at first light to have a look."

"Oh, good, can I come along?" Shadow asked.

"Erm, yes, of course, I would like that," replied Rambo.

Shadow took a last look around at the friends he thought he had lost and closed his eyes with a heavy sigh. "Good night, everyone, good night," he whispered, as he drifted off to sleep.

Chapter 4
The Killing Begins

It was just before sunup when Shadow and Rambo reached the pen at the bottom of the hill. What they found when they got there was very hard to believe. The sheep were huddled against one another in the pen. They looked terrified. As he looked at the flock, some of them had large patches of thick, dark, matted blood spreading across their chests. There was a dead lamb in the corner, and most were crying; all were shaking and hungry.

"Baaaah, baaaah."

Shadow looked across at the ewe making all the noise. It was the same old ewe he had spoken to last time they visited the pen. Rambo walked around the outside of the pen to where the tiny body of the dead lamb lay, still with its umbilical cord trailing from its stomach. "You poor, poor, tiny thing." He looked up to see its mother standing nearby. Rambo asked her what happened.

"The Menflock came. They took out most of the lambs but missed my newborn. She was crushed while they pushed and shoved us about. I couldn't get to her."

He knew it was too late to help the little one, but maybe they could help the others. He looked around for Shadow, who was still talking to the old ewe.

"They came in here and pushed sharp needles into our necks to take blood from us for testing. Antibodies, they said they were testing for, antibodies. As you can see from the state of us, some of them were not very good at it." The blood was all over the pen, the sheep, and the floor. One or two of the sheep looked very weak.

"Shadow, what are we going to do?" asked Rambo.

Shadow thought for a few moments, then the old ewe spoke again, "There is nothing you can do; they are coming back this morning to kill every one of us regardless of these antibodies, as a precaution, they said, as a precaution." It no longer seemed to matter if they had foot and mouth or not; they were all to die anyway. The old ewe spoke again, "I'm sorry I didn't listen to you yesterday. I was wrong. We should have tried to run away."

Shadow ran off to the side of the pen. He thought that if he could chew the bailing twine as he did before, some of them might get away. To his horror, he found that the Menflock had replaced the twine with a big metal chain. It wrapped around the posts again and again. There was no chance of opening the gate. He didn't want to go back to the old ewe with the bad news, so he looked for other ways of escape. There were none to be found. Finally, he returned to her. "I'm sorry," he said, "I can't get you out." Silence fell over the group while they came to terms with what seemed to be inevitable. All the sheep were to be killed, generations of ancient flocks to be wiped out in just one day. Shadow and Rambo turned away and began the long climb up the hill knowing they would not be returning to the pen. What would be the point?

The rest of the family waited patiently for them to return. The sun had been up for quite a while, yet the pen was still in shadow. Eventually, it began to shine on the east face of the hill. The long, drawn-out shadow gradually receded as the sun rose yet higher. The sun was very strong that morning, which was just as well, as when Shadow and Rambo were about fifty metres from the top of the hill, the Menflock arrived at the pen. The sun shone right into the eyes of the Menflock. If they did look up toward them, they would be blinded by the sun, so they were safe.

"Okay then," said one of the Menflock, "let's get on with this. We're paid by the head, you know. What have we got? Two captive bolt guns, a big box of .22 blanks, and a bundle of pithing rods. Yep, we're set."

"Why do you need two weapons? There's only you here to use them," asked a young assistant from the local army barracks. The army was involved mainly with logistics, controlling vehicles, deliveries, and suchlike, but some of the squaddies were given more frontline duties as is usually the case.

"We got a lot of killing to do here today, and I'll need to swap them over or else they gonna overheat. I told you we're paid by the head, and we ain't slowing down. Time's money, lad, time's money, and time's a-wastin'. Ay, vet, are you coming in here to help or not?" shouted the man. His voice was hardly heard over the cries of frightened sheep. "These dumb animals won't hold it against ya, I promise; they all be dead soon." He laughed and turned away. He was so hardened by the life of killing that he smiled, turned to his young assistant, and said in a low tone, "He won't come in here, lad. Don't like getting their 'ands dirty, they don't."

He was right. The vet looked at the pen and at the poor animals within it and picked up his clipboard. "Love to help, but I've got to do the paperwork. Maybe next time."

The slaughter man chuckled to his young assistant, "Told ya so, matey. Not got the stomach for hard work, them sort."

The slaughter man drew a shiny silver pistol from its pouch, slid a .22 calibre blank into the breach of the weapon, and snapped it shut. "Now, lad, you stay behind me at all times. If you come into view of the corner of my eye just once, I will kick the living crap out of you. That's your warning; you don't get no other." He was worried about injuring the lad if he got in the way. Just a few days before, one of the Menflock had been injured when he got in the way of the weapon. "You only pith the sheep behind me. You 'ere me lad? Behind me." He looked at the lad for a sign that he understood the instruction.

"Okay," said the lad, "but I still don't know what to do."

The man pointed to a bundle of blue rods lying on the floor of the pen. "Get me one of those."

The squaddie pulled out a long, blue rod, about six hundred millimetres long, and handed it to the man. The man turned, and there was a pause while he decided which of the group was to die first. *Bang!* She dropped and rolled onto her side. Steam was rising from the hole made in her skull. She was lying there unconscious but not yet dead. The worst was yet to come. The slaughter man stood over the ewe. The lad moved toward her to learn his task. The slaughter man bent forward and lifted the limp head of the helpless ewe. With his index finger, he located the hole made in the ewe's head by the weapon's firing pin. "You watching, lad?"

Gingerly, the lad leaned over.

"Just get the pith inside the skull, but be sure to aim for the back of the head. Don't let it go toward the mouth, or it won't work. Then when you are sure it's hard in place, pump it in and out real hard, real hard, to mash the back of the brain. When the animal stops kicking, it's dead! But," he continued, "to make sure, lift its head and look it right in the eye. Look, lad, look!" He looked at the lad, who had turned a very strange colour. The lad looked into the sheep's eye. "Look deep, lad, deep." The young soldier looked intently for something, but at this time, he was not sure what to look for. As he looked deeply into the eyes of this doomed animal, he saw the sparkle of its eye turn to an opaque grey. He turned to the slaughter man, lost for words. He had just watched the life drain away.

"Now lad, last thing, put your finger in her eye. You need to check her eye. If the pupil still moves when you touch it, you gotta start again."

The young soldier stood silent.

"Well, come on! Get hold of another pith, your turn."

This man is obviously insane, thought the squaddie, but with a knot in his stomach, he was ready.

Click, click, bang! Another one dropped to the earth. Click, click, bang! And another. Bang, bang, bang, bang, there seemed to be no end to the carnage as sheep fell. Steam was rising into the air, and the young soldier was leaning over each and every one of the desperate animals, each kicking, contorting, and finally, dying. When he looked into the eyes of each ewe, he saw the bright sparkle of life fade away, giving way to an opaque grey as the animal died. "If you're not sure, boy, just touch her eyeball. Go on! If her pupil moves, do it again."

"Oh my word," he cried. The boy could stand this no longer. He threw down the remaining pith rods and jumped over the rail. "Stuff this," he said. "Stuff this. I didn't join the army for this."

"What's up, boy? We've just got started," shouted the slaughter man as the lad walked off in the direction of the power washer to remove his blood-soaked whites.

"Oh, stuff this," he shouted back. "And stuff you an' all. You're crazy!" He continued on his way.

Just then, a large, green Land Rover appeared in the car park below. "Me Badger Boy mates! Rooster, Mark, get up here; I need you boys." Rooster and Mark had worked with him in the south and were no strangers to any aspect of the task. After all, they were Badger Boys; they killed for a living.

"Hey, Dave, where were you at breakfast?" Just a normal day at work!

"I'll tell you later," replied Dave. "Just get togged up and pith for me, will you? The army has just retreated." Dave continued to drop the sheep one by one, and after a few minutes, the two Badger Boys, Rooster and Mark, climbed into the pen and pithed and pithed until not a sheep was alive. All three sat at one end of the pen, their ears ringing from the intense noise that had now abruptly stopped. Breathing heavily, they scanned the mass of bodies, looking for signs of life. There were none.

"Just another day at the office, hey?" said Rooster.

They all laughed.

Shadow and Rambo were now safely back in the dip on the top of the hill. "What do you think?" said Tom. "Is all going to be okay?"

"We didn't stick around to see what happened, but we think they're all dead. There's no noise, and look, a big machine is moving toward the pen." The machine was a Manitou. It had huge, spiked jaws on the front. They couldn't see how their friends died, but they could see their bodies being shovelled up like leaves by the big machine and carried toward the road to a waiting wagon. Who knew what would happen to the bodies then? One thing was for sure: They were dead, and if captured, so would they be. All of them seemed to lose more than friends on that fateful day.

In a very matter-of-fact way, Tom gave instructions to the group. "We travel at night. There is no way we can afford to be seen."

Everyone agreed. It was going to be a long day. They were trapped in the dip during daylight with the noise of the machine scooping up the bodies of their friends. Gwen came over to Tom and lay against his broad chest. "Oh, Tom, we're all in this together. We will all work together. Remember, we're the W.M.S.F., the Welsh Mountain Special Flock."

Tom felt rather foolish about it all now, but as he looked around at his family, he thought, *That might be the only chance to keep them alive, so yes, let's get tough or die.*

The sun was quite warm that day, and eventually, the noise stopped almost as suddenly as it began. Rambo raised his head carefully over the ridge. The pen was empty. The entire side of the hill was empty save for themselves. Shadow gave some thought to the forest, and whether the Badger Boys returned there or not, it wasn't safe to stay on the hill. Dusk finally arrived, and after a good day of rest, the twins were ready for the long haul to the forest.

"Okay, everyone, get some fresh mud on those lily-white butts, and let's move out," said Tom.

Shadow took point, and Rambo brought up the rear as assigned. The twins were in the middle with Slight on one side and Mother on the other.

Tom was in front of Gwen and the twins' group, monitoring Shadow's activities ahead. "Let's go."

Chapter 5

The Journey Begins

As planned, they stuck to the high ground along Craig Gwaun Taf and Rhlw Yr Ysgyfarnog to Craig Fan Ddu. All was going well, even though it would be a long trip for the twins. They kept in a tight group, as Shadow had told them that it was very steep on both sides for the first half of the journey. After that, it was a gentle slope on the right from Cefn Cul and along Craig Fan Ddu, but the left was still very dangerous for the little ones. It was a very eerie trip with no sign of any other sheep. It was as if they were the only animals left in the world. They then heard the sound of an owl screeching. This did make them jump a little, but at least they no longer felt alone. Then came the swift flyby of bats swishing this way and that, making an airborne meal of those pesky flying insects that kept biting them.

"We must be near the water and the forest now," whispered Tom. "I can't see Shadow for the moment, but I'm sure he's okay," he said, trying to reassure himself.

Shadow re-appeared ahead of them saying, "Not far now. The pile of stones is just a bit further. Just a bit more."

Mother looked at the twins. They looked very tired, but they were still going strong. *Such strength in ones so young,* she thought.

Little did she realise at this time how much strength these little lambs would need if they were to survive what was to befall them all in the near future.

"Look! Look! What's that?" asked Rambo. A large, imposing object seemed to loom high in front of them.

"Don't worry," said Shadow, "it's the pile of stones. This is where we turn east into the safety of the woodland."

It was just before sunup. They all gathered at the pile of stones and turned to the east.

"Oh my, it's beautiful," said Gwen. The shimmering waters of the reservoir glistened beneath them to the northeast. A bright reflection of the moon made it seem as though it were dancing just for them. A strange, rhythmic, whooshing noise drifted toward them from the forest as the trees seemed to join in with the dance.

All were silent watching this spectacle with their heads waving from side to side in unison with the trees. They had never seen such a sight. Shadow was the only one that had ever seen trees up close before or such a large body of water.

"Hello!"

They all turned and looked at one another.

"Hello!"

They looked at Bethan and smiled. They all thought she had said "hello" to the water beneath.

"I said hello. Are you not listening to me?" the voice said once more.

"It wasn't me; I didn't say anything," said Bethan.

"It was me," said the voice.

They all looked toward Tom, and to their surprise, a tiny bat was hanging upside down on Tom's large, curled horn.

"It's a bat," said Gwen. "There is a bat hanging from your left horn, Tom."

Tom turned his head.

"Wey hey," the bat squealed as Tom spun his head. "Steady on, big fella. I'm only small, you know."

"Sorry," said Tom, "but I can't see you there."

The bat edged her way along the horn, swinging gently as she went. The others just watched this unusual occurrence, but nobody said a word.

"There, how's that?" The bat was swinging gently just a few inches from Tom's eye. "You must be able to see me now."

Tom's eyes moved left and right in time to the swinging of the little bat hanging from his horn.

"Not very good eyesight you guys have you?" the bat said. "I can't see much at all, but I can still see better than you lot."

"I wish you wouldn't swing like that; it's making me feel quite sick," said Tom.

"Oh, sorry," said the bat as she widened her grip on Tom's horn to steady herself a little. "There, is that better?" asked the little visitor.

"Yes, thank you," replied Tom.

The others looked at this spectacle, and in one gentle movement, their heads turned clockwise to see the little creature right way up or upside down or, hmmm, anyway. The moment lingered for a little while until Gwen said, "We have never spoken to a bat before. Why are you here?"

At this point, the other sheep realised how silly they all must have looked with their heads upside down and turned back to their upright positions.

The bat responded Gwen's question, "We have heard that the Menflock have turned against you. Is that true?"

"Yes," said Gwen. "It would seem so. Why do you ask? And please excuse our ignorance, but we didn't know that bats could talk."

"That's okay," said the bat. "We have never spoken to you before because you were friends of the Menflock, and we're not. They have been cruel to us also in the past, but in our view, your enemy's enemy is your ally, and so with permission from the high council, I am allowed to speak with you."

They all settled down near the pile of stones for a rest, and Shadow began to explain to the bat what had happened on the hill so far.

"Hmm. Yes. Hmmm. I see," murmured the bat as she listened intently to the tale so far. "Okay," said the bat, "we can help you a little. If you wish, I will be your messenger. I saw that the dog there, Shadow, runs ahead to scout the route. Well, I can relay messages between you both and look even farther around the area if that would help."

"That would be a great help," replied Shadow, and they all thanked the bat for her offer.

"Can I ask you something, little bat?" asked Rambo.

"If you wish, little ram."

"My name is Rambo. Rambo!" He didn't take kindly to being regarded as a little ram anymore. The last couple of days had changed that forever.

"Okay, Rambo, ask away."

"Why are you enemies of the Menflock? What did they do to you?"

They had all wondered this, but Rambo was the only one bold enough to ask. Gwen butted in, "Rambo, that's none of our business. I'm sorry, bat, you don't have to answer that."

"No, that's okay," the bat replied. "I have no objection. It might help you realise who you are up against with these Menflock."

The bat let go of Tom's horn and flew to the pile of rocks a few feet away. "Us pipistrelle or flittermouse bats, as I prefer, don't generally hang free like most bats. We prefer to cling to a vertical surface like this pile of rocks to get comfy. Ahh, that's better. Oh, by the way, my name is Pippa." The little bat yawned and stretched her tiny wings. She explained that she was woken early from her winter sleep to speak to them. By rights, she should be asleep for another few weeks at least.

Pippa began to recount her story. "When I was young, my father hung me on a rock, very similar to this one actually or maybe a little rounder."

"We get the idea, Pippa," said Gwen.

"Yes, okay, well, he told me that Menflock like to kill. If they stop killing each other for a while, they kill animals. If they have a day off, they go out to kill some more for fun: birds, rabbits, foxes, hares. You name it; they will find a reason to kill it. Many years ago, a great war was raging right across the world. Millions of Menflock were dying at the hands of other Menflock. They had especially cunning ones who dreamt up all sorts of ways to cause damage to the Menflock on the other side. Well, one day, they went to a cave in a place called the Carlsbad Caverns in New Mexico looking to take some free-tailed bats, called domed-plated mastiff bats, to use in their army."

"Tom," whispered Gwen, "where is New Mexico?"

"Oh, erm, I think it's about three hills away," he replied, not wanting her to know that he didn't have a clue where it was. "Carry on," said Tom.

Pippa continued, "They captured thousands of the free-tailed bats because they are very strong even though they are very small. They have the ability to extend their wings to increase their effective size down along the tail. See, look, mine is fixed in place; theirs can move up and down. It makes their wings bigger so they can carry more weight. Good, hey! Anyway, once caught, they were put into big crates. Then the Menflock lowered the temperature in the crates to forty degrees Fahrenheit. At this temperature, the bats pass out, remain dormant, and don't need feeding. Tests found that they could carry three times their body weight, so little one-ounce, incendiary time bombs were strapped to their chests. The bombs were larger than the bats themselves.

"Big crates with thousands of these captured, trapped bats inside were carried in aeroplanes high into the sky and then thrown out to fall onto their intended targets. The little bats were released from the crates on the way down to the ground. As they fell, the temperature rose. It's nice and warm in Mexico, you know. Hmmmmmmm, yes, lovely and warm. Well, as they woke from their enforced sleep, they flew out of the crates in panic. When they came close to the ground, they hid amongst buildings spread over an area of maybe twenty miles and tried desperately to remove the harnesses. Some may have done so, but many thousands died, being burned alive by the exploding packages strapped to them."

The others were stunned to silence by this awful tale.

"Fortunately, though," she continued, "when they tested the effect on a town close to the caves, some of the bats flew to the local air base at Carlsbad and set fire to it. Hee-hee! Imagine that. Hee-hee! They set fire to their own air base. How dumb is that, hey. Project X-ray they called it. We're not too sure how many times it was used or even if it was used at all after that, but it was only stopped because the Menflock made terrifyingly big bombs and used them to wipe out thousands of Menflock. I told you Menflock are no friends of bat-kind."

"There goes any chance I had of a good night's sleep," said Bethan.

Gwen turned to her and held her close; she had thought she was asleep. She looked at the others and felt as though the whole world was against them.

Tom turned to Pippa, saying, "Glad you are with us, Pip."

"You're welcome, I'm sure. Hey, I have to go now; it's almost sunup," the bat said. "We only fly at night."

The bat fluttered away, shouting back at the group, "Don't worry, I will be back tonight after sundown. I will ask the birds where you are." Her little, squeaky voice faded into the air, and she vanished.

"The birds! Do the birds speak as well, Father?" asked Rambo.

"I guess we will find out soon, won't we?" he replied.

Shadow turned to Tom, "I think I will check out the woodland before we go in."

Whoosh, whoosh. Pippa had returned. "Stay away from the water, far away from the water." She swished this way and that. "Big, hairy monster, biiiig, hairy monster. Will explain tonight." And once again, she was gone.

"I think I could have done without hearing that," said Slight, who had not spoken a word since she was told of the death of her partner.

Tom looked at her. "Yes, I think I could too."

"Ha, ha, ha, ha," Shadow laughed. "Hairy monster, indeed. Let's just get through what we can see for the moment and not worry about hairy monsters." Shadow ran off to do recon in the forest to the east. As he ran, he recalled one of the stories that the farmer used to relate about a hairy monster. The tale had been told for generations in Brecon, but he didn't want to tell the others that, not yet anyway.

The twins were again nuzzled into their mother, taking warm milk, with Slight at her side.

Rambo and Tom were silent. "How am I ever to protect my family from such evil as these Menflock?" Tom refused to think of the added possibility of a hairy monster.

Chapter 6
Into the Forest

SHADOW knew he didn't have a great deal of time before sunup. They would all need to be well hidden in the forest by the time any Men-flock came back onto the hill at daylight. Gwen looked toward the forest. The trees were still swaying, making a swishing noise as they waved gently from side to side.

"I've never slept in a forest before," Gwen said to Slight.

"No, neither have I, but don't worry. I will help you with the twins."

Shadow was gone for about an hour, though it seemed a lot longer to those left waiting for his return. Pads pounding on the well-trodden track, Shadow appeared in the distance. "My, that dog can run," observed Tom.

On his return, Shadow gave his report. "All is clear, but we will need to be quick because the sun is almost upon us, and I can hear vehicles and voices on the wind from the bottom of the valley."

It was a very misty morning. The air was cold, and Shadow's panting let out long wisps of white breath as it billowed from his mouth. No comment was made on this as they were all well used to the rigours of cold weather. They took their assigned positions in the group and began to walk the short distance from the pile of stones down the steep hill into the forest.

The trees didn't look so friendly so close up; in fact, they looked quite angry that this little band of refugees was invading their space.

Finally, they were all inside the forest. Shadow informed the group, "If we're all very quiet, we can walk along this track. It goes deep into the forest." That was where Shadow had previously seen the Badger Boys and witnessed the unfortunate plight of one tumbling down the slope. He thought it best not to tell the others he had seen them, nor did he think it wise to explain who they were, as they were not there any longer and so didn't present an immediate problem. So long as they were all quiet, they would be able to hear them or any other Menflock if they returned to the forest.

The sun was now up, and streams of light came through the canopy, lighting up patches of ground as they went. They could hear a strong breeze but couldn't feel it at all as it buffeted the trees at the edge of the forest. The seclusion of the forest made them feel a little safer for the time being, and they were glad of its help. "Everything seems so close," whispered Tom. "I can't see more than a few metres. How are we supposed to see anyone approaching?"

Shadow turned to Tom, "If you can only see a few metres, anyone looking for us can also only see a few metres, and with all this dense cover, we can drop into the furrows between the trees and escape."

"I suppose so," responded Tom. He turned to the rest of the family, saying, "We all need to be very quiet in here so we can hear any other sheep that may be hiding in here." He didn't wish to frighten them by telling them that they may come across Menflock on the track. He was still not aware of the previous presence of the Badger Boys that Shadow had seen prior to them reaching the forest.

As they continued, Gwen looked around. "Not much grass to eat in here, Tom."

He turned toward her, "Hmm, I noticed that, but there is some on the edge of the track; that will have to do for now."

Gwen was right; this forest was a tightly packed pine plantation, and very little if anything would grow beneath it. As they ventured deeper into the forest, it grew darker and darker until the little strip of sky above the track provided the only light. They weren't at all used to this enclosed space. The sky was so big on home hill, stretching as far as the world went in every direction, but here, they only saw a narrow strip over their heads and a thin, green line of very acidic-tasting grass along its edge. "Not likely to find any discarded sandwiches in here either," said Shadow, as his tummy rumbled. It had been two days since he had eaten any food. He turned to Tom, "We need to look at our basic needs, shelter, water, and food."

Tom turned to him, "I agree. Do you feel strong enough to scout ahead?"

"Yes, but let's stop on the track for a while so that you sheep can feed on this grass. When you have finished, we will leave the track and find an L.U.P."

"Okay," replied Tom, looking a little vague. "Just one question," Tom said quietly. "What's an L.U.P.?"

"Lay-Up Point," replied Shadow. "You know, somewhere to lay up and wait."

"Oh, right," whispered Tom. "Wait for what?" He was a little worried at this comment.

"Somewhere safe, Tom, that's all, just somewhere safe."

"Okay, oh, yes, I know what you mean."

Tom turned to the others. "Okay, we're going to stop here to find an L.U.P. for a little R and R."

Everyone fell silent. Gwen gave him the look, you know, the one that needs no words, the slight tilting of the head, a flicker of an agitated eyelid, the look that said, "If I have to ask what you mean, I will make you suffer in ways not yet invented."

Tom, of course, felt this hidden threat in the pit of his stomach.

"Sorry, what I meant to say was that we're going into the trees to have a rest, but first Shadow is going to keep stag, that is, errrm, I mean, guard, while we eat some grass."

With a wry grin, the moment passed, and they all looked into the forest. "It's so dark in there, Mother," said little Bethan. "What about monsters? What about the hairy monster that Pippa the bat told us about?"

Gwen turned to the frightened little lamb. "Don't worry, Bethan. What hairy monster would think of bothering us with your father to look after us?"

Tom stopped chewing but didn't lift his head. He was a little unsure of himself of late and, as usual, couldn't tell if Gwen was being sarcastic or not, but he let the comment slide by, pretending not to hear. Bethan looked at her father and was more than sure he was just the biggest protector in the world. She smiled at him, wagged her little tail, smiled once more, and leant against her mother.

Shadow stood guard a few metres away as the others ate the not-so-pleasant grass. When it was apparent that they had all eaten enough, Tom spoke, "Okay, we need to get into the trees and find somewhere comfortable to rest until we have decided what to do next."

Shadow returned to the group. "There is a small stream just ahead. If we make our way toward it, you can enter the forest there. I think we will be okay there; it's warm, dry, and you have grass to eat. I will have to look elsewhere for food."

They made their way along the track to the small stream and turned off to the left into the trees. They only had to go a few meters to be completely concealed by the sheer density of the trees. A thick bed of pine needles covered the floor, making the ground as soft as wool. "It's so soft," said Slight. "This is wonderful."

The twins were running up and down the furrows between the rows of trees. "Weeeeee." They rolled down the slopes. Boing,

boing, boing. "It's bouncy, Mother," said Hailwen. "Look." They bounced up and down, their big, floppy ears trying to keep up with their grinning faces.

"Shhhhh, shhhhhh, get down, stay still," insisted Shadow.

A noise in the distance seemed to be getting louder: "A quad, it's a quad," said Rambo, "and it's coming in our direction."

"Nobody make a sound," continued Tom. "Lie low, and keep very, very still."

It was indeed a quad, and it was heading right along the track they had been walking. The roar of the engine was getting close, and every now and then, the machine would stop. The man stood high on the footrests to look into the forest. Everyone's hearts were pounding. It was one of those times when even the sound of your own heart seemed too loud, and they were afraid it would give them away. He came closer to their L.U.P. and stopped again. Yet again, he stood high on the machine to get a better look. He seemed to be looking right at them, and for an everlasting moment, he stretched even higher. Rambo thought, *He'll get a cramp in his bum, stretching like that.* He recalled how unpleasant his experience was and only wished that this man would get cramp in his bum and go away.

The man finally sat down again on his machine and continued along the track. A group sigh was so strong that it was almost deafening. "Well, it's a good job we came in here when we did," stated Slight.

"A good job, indeed," replied Tom.

The roar of the quad gradually faded into the distance. The woodland no longer felt frightening; it had given them food, shelter, cover, and had even saved their lives. Yes, this was a good L.U.P. Close by, the gentle trickling sound assured them that they were near water. Shadow took a long drink and sat amongst the others.

The day was getting weary, the sun was beginning to dip, and it seemed to go dark very early in the forest. The twins were well fed and fast asleep. Shadow, Tom, and Rambo discussed what to do next.

"Shadow, are you strong enough to go out and scout?" Tom asked.

"Yes, I am, but I will need food tomorrow. I have a suggestion."

Tom and Rambo listened carefully as Shadow convinced them that he and Rambo should carry on south in the direction of Merthyr Tydfil. They were to visit the lowland sheep grazing just north of Merthyr to ask for their assistance. "Surely this foot and mouth thing can't be down there also, can it?" Shadow hoped.

"Only one way to find out, I suppose," said Tom. "It's going to rain tonight. I can feel it in my horns. Have a rest before you both go, and we will see if the bat comes back tonight. Maybe she will have a suggestion."

The three agreed: Rambo and Shadow were to go to Merthyr the next morning.

Tom was right! It rained very hard that night. Little raindrops seemed to collect until they were large enough to break through the canopy above and fall like liquid rocks on the sheep below. The twins crawled deep under Mother to hide from these exploding rocks, and Slight moved close to give them extra cover. "Let's hope we don't have too much rain while we're in here," said Slight. They all looked at her and nodded in agreement. The rain slowly stopped, and the weary group of refugees fell fast asleep, dreaming of Home Hill, strange goings-on in the grass, and long, sunny summer days. It all seemed so far away, but at least they were safe and together.

Pippa didn't come that evening, but very early the following morning, she fluttered in as promised. The twins were still asleep as she flew in, swishing this way and that way, darting here, darting there. Finally, she landed on the trunk of a tree next to the group. "Sorry, I'm late. Lots of bugs tonight; I'm fit to bust. I can eat maybe three thousand in one night, you know, but I couldn't eat another one. Well, this is a nice little place you have. Plenty of room for entertaining. Hmm, yes, very nice."

"Hello, Pippa," said Tom. "We thought you weren't coming."

"I promised I would come, didn't I? Have you ever heard of a bat breaking a promise?" she replied.

"Come to think of it, no, I haven't," said Tom.

"Have faith, oh great, woolly one. I am here now."

They told the bat what they had planned, and she agreed to be their communication link, flying back and forth between the two groups every night to bring news.

Pippa told them that word on the bat-vine was that a white calf called Phoenix was in league with some Menflock in Devon that were fighting to stop the killing.

"Maybe we should go and find this Phoenix," said Rambo.

"First things first," replied Tom. "Let's just look in the valley; it would be very difficult to travel any distance. I have heard there is a huge body of water in the south. It would be impossible for any of us to cross this into the unknown lands."

Pippa continued to speak, "During my travels through this forest, I discovered a place where the Menflock don't go. In fact," she said, "I live there. Why don't you come and stay with me?"

"We might do that, Pippa, but we will wait here for Shadow and Rambo to return from the valley before we move. That is, unless it becomes unsafe."

"Okay," said Pippa. The bat explained to them exactly where she lived, just in case they needed to move to a safer location. She bade them farewell and fluttered off once more, "Till tomorrow, then. Bye, keep low." And she was gone.

"Well, it's time," stated Shadow. "Are you sure you are up for this, Rambo? This will be dangerous!"

"I'm no tourist," replied Rambo. "If they want a war, I'll give them a war they won't believe."

Tom looked at Shadow. "Keep your eye on him, will you? I think he's a bit strung out."

"He will be fine. He's tough," replied Shadow.

Chapter 7
The Group Splits Up

WHEN Shadow and Rambo began their journey, it was not quite sunrise. The first part of the journey was under the cover of the forest, and therefore, they could relax a little as they moved in the dense cover.

"Shadow," said Rambo, "can I ask you a question?"

"You just did," said Shadow.

Rambo contemplated this comment for a moment until Shadow said, "Yes, Rambo, go ahead. What would you like to know?"

Rambo, still looking a little puzzled, continued, "The bat, Pippa, spoke of a hairy monster. What are we going to do if we meet a hairy monster?"

"Nothing, he won't harm us. Don't worry."

"Do you mean to say it's true, that there really is a hairy monster?" Rambo asked.

"Yes, but he is angry with the Menflock, not with sheep or dogs."

Shadow had spent many evenings sitting by the fireside while the farmer told Welsh folklore tales of fairies, ladies of the lake, mysterious caves, and yes indeed, one big, hairy monster living in the lake.

"Legend has it," he continued, "a farmer used to go down to the lake. Llyn Safadon, I think it was called. The farmer had some lambs he had bought at a fair. They were grazing by the lake. Each time he went down to the lake, he saw three beautiful maidens by the water's edge. He tried to catch one of them, but they all escaped into the water to vanish, but on one occasion, before they vanished beneath the waters, he proposed marriage to one of them. She turned to him and, to his surprise, consented. They married soon after but on the understanding that, if they were to have three disputes, she would leave him and return to the lake from where she came. Anyway, as such is the way with Menflock, three disputes eventually occurred, and the maiden of the lake, true to her stated promise, returned to the water. The young farmer was so upset by this that he and his friends began to dig a deep furrow to drain the lake in order to get his bride back. As they began to dig, a huge, hairy monster rose from the water. It was terrible to look at. It stormed toward them shouting, *"If I get no quiet in my place, I shall drown the whole town of Brecon!"*

"What happened?" said Rambo.

"Well," continued Shadow, "Brecon is still there, isn't it? I guess they thought better of it and stopped digging."

"So it's true then; a hairy monster does live in the lake," Rambo said, looking for some response from Shadow that would help him to dismiss such a claim.

"Afraid so, Rambo, but as I said, it is angry with the Menflock, not with us."

Rambo mused over the tale for quite some time. "If there is a monster in one lake, there are probably monsters in all the lakes. What a dangerous world this is outside our protected little hill."

They had travelled quite some distance by the time the tale was told. Rambo had given great contemplation to this hairy monster and wondered if they could make contact with him. He might help them fight the Menflock.

He turned to Shadow. "That would solve a lot of our problems, wouldn't it?"

Shadow, not having a clue what he was on about, stopped. "What would?" he said in response.

"I was thinking about the hairy monster. If we could get in touch with him, he might just carry out his threat and drown all the Menflock in Brecon."

Shadow was horrified. "Don't you let your mother hear you say things like that. Sheep are one of the few creatures that have never deliberately killed anything. Anyway, if you are brave enough to wake up a sleeping, hairy monster, you are on your own. I won't be anywhere near you when you do."

Rambo felt a little ashamed for making this suggestion. He was about to apologise to Shadow.

"Get down!" Shadow had seen two Menflock in white suits in the fields ahead of them. They were just clear of the forest edge, and so from this point on, they had to be on full alert. "We need to follow the field edge and rain ditches from now on. Stay very low and follow me."

They crawled gingerly along a half-filled drainage ditch. It was so cold, muddy, and very slippery. After they had passed the danger of being spotted by the two Menflock, they slowly and carefully raised their heads above the edge of the ditch. They could see sheep in the field ahead.

"Look," said Rambo, "they are not penned up, and the grass looks really good from here. Maybe we will all be safe down there."

Shadow was not so optimistic. "Let's make our way around the edge of the field and talk to the sheep on the other side. We can ask them what they know of the foot and mouth."

It was hard going travelling in the ditch, but they eventually got to the other side of the field. On turning the last corner, they spotted another sheep in the ditch. It was a few hundred metres away, but it was definitely a sheep. Shadow raised his head to check their position as they continued forward toward the sheep. As they got nearer, they noticed that the sheep in the ditch was upside down, but her bony legs were waving around. "Whatever can be the matter with her?" said Shadow. They moved toward her to find that, yes indeed, she was upside down. Her little legs had been waving about because she had slipped in the mud and fallen into the ditch. She had landed on her back and was drowning.

"Oh no, we've got to get her up. Quickly, quickly. Shadow, help me, please," cried Rambo.

Shadow had seen this type of thing happen before. He took hold of a big mouthful of Rambo's wool and gently pulled him away from the ewe. "It's no good; she is dead. There is no way we could lift her up." Eventually, her bony legs just twitched a few more times and then stopped. She was gone. Rambo was shaking with sheer stress, and he backed away to stand beside Shadow.

Shadow raised his head above the ditch. Just a few meters away, there was an old ewe standing in the field. Rambo slithered in the mud alongside her. What he saw was just as horrific as the death of the old ewe. The field was waterlogged from the torrential rain that Tom had accurately forecast. The field was awash with slimy, grey-brown mud and had very little grass on it at all. A young lamb was stuck firm in the mud just a few metres from where its mother had fallen into the ditch. They knew that its mother was dead. The mud in the field completely covered the legs of the ewe, and the little lamb was just about enveloped in it.

"Oh gosh, Shadow, what are we to do?"

Shadow looked at Rambo. "We will do what we came here to do. We will talk to the sheep." The sun was setting, and Shadow said, "We can't spend the night here. If we do, we will soon be dead too. There is an old barn over there. I think we should go into it to spend the night."

They were both shaking with the cold, and it was agreed to be the best thing to do. The barn proved to be a very good choice indeed. It was warm, dry, and used as a food store, not just for hay, but there, lying in the corner, was a large bag of dry dog food. "Now this is a find! Ha, ha, look at all this. The farmer must leave this here for his dogs when they are working up here."

They both tucked into their meals and bedded down into a broken bale of hay high in the rooftop of the barn. After a while, the shivering from the cold began to slow. Just occasional flickers of their warming muscles reminded them of how cold they had been. It had been many hours since they had food and shelter, and thoughts turned to the rest of the family in the forest.

"That was a good spot we found in the forest, wasn't it, Shadow?"

"Yes, it was."

They both felt a little guilty about their good fortune in the barn, but they also knew that, if it were not for the find, they would soon be in trouble, big trouble. The following morning, a sharp ray of sunlight beamed into the barn through a tiny hole in the eves, striking Shadow on his face. They lay there for a little while and thought it best to eat again before going about their business in the fields outside.

Unknown to them, Pippa had flown in during the night and was fast asleep, hanging against the gable end of the barn about two metres above their heads. Rambo saw her first. "Look, Shadow, it's Pippa. I wonder when she got here."

Shadow looked up toward the little bat. "I don't know, but she must be very tired. Let's not wake her yet. Let's get some food down us first, and then we will ask her for news of the others." They enjoyed the comforts of the barn a little while longer, trying to muster up the physical and mental strength and courage to face the day ahead.

"Hello, you guys. How are you?" the little voice asked. Pippa stretched her little wings and yawned.

"Hello, Pippa," replied Shadow. "We're fine. How on earth did you find us here?"

"It wasn't easy; I'll tell you. I flew all night—you have travelled such a long way. I will spend the day here sleeping and get back up north tonight. Tom and the others asked me to tell you that they are okay. They are thinking of coming to stay with me in my old barn in the forest; it should be safe there, and there is grass to eat. They are hoping you have good news of the lowland sheep."

Shadow and Rambo looked at one another. Do they tell them about the plight of the sheep seen the previous day, or not? "Well," started Shadow, "we have not yet spoken to the sheep down here, but we will let them know as soon as we can. The weather has been bad, so it slowed us a little, but not to worry, we're both fine."

"Okay," said Pippa, "I will tell them tonight."

Pippa flew back up to the gable wall and landed alongside another pipistrelle bat. "Don't mind if I kip here for the day, do you?" she asked.

"Not at all," replied the second little bat. "Where did you come from?"

Pippa told the story so far to the bat, who said she would be more than willing to help in the relay if needed. "Oh, that would be great. I am at my limit here, and if these guys go much farther, I won't be able to reach them at all."

The two bats got to know one another a little better over a supper of juicy bugs, and then, with a tiny flutter of wings, they settled down for a good day's sleep.

Shadow and Rambo looked up at the bats.

"Sweet dreams, Pippa," whispered Rambo as they left the comfort of the barn once more. It was a bright day. The birds were singing and busy making nests for their young ones soon to arrive. It was so hard to believe that their world seemed to be in such a mess. They looked hesitantly at the cold, muddy drainage ditch and, with deep sighs, slipped down the bank into it so as not to be seen.

"Brrrrr, that's cold," remarked Rambo.

"Yes, it is," agreed Shadow, "but let's get moving; we have a lot to do."

They made their way along the drainage ditch once more toward the dead ewe. When they got near to her, they carefully raised their heads to see her lamb still trapped in the thick, cold, slimy mud.

"She's not moving," whispered Shadow. "I think she is dead."

The little lamb had suffered terribly during the night and had finally died from the cold or hunger or maybe just the stress of her ordeal. Whatever the reason was, the result was the same. Rambo felt numb, angry that this little lamb could be abandoned to such a miserable fate. "We should carry on from here to talk to the ewes on the other side of the field. We need to know what is going on." They couldn't help being glad that they had left the others in the safety of the forest. The twins would have surely died in this terrible place.

It took a good while to reach the sheep across the field. When they got there, they could hear the cries of young and old alike. What a terrible state they were in. Shadow turned to Rambo, "I want you to wait here while I go and speak to them."

Rambo objected, "But I will be fine."

"No, you won't! Think about it! They are stuck; you will get stuck. I am lighter than you, and I don't get waterlogged; no wool, you see."

Rambo, still willing to prove his bravery, said, "I'm not frightened to go."

Shadow looked at the young ram. "I never imagined that you were, nor did I question your bravery, but remember this: Never confuse cowardice with caution. If I were not confident in your abilities, you would not be here with me."

Rambo felt a lot better and tried to remember what Shadow had said, "Never confuse cowardice with caution. Hmm, I like that one."

Shadow stayed low to the ground, edging slowly toward the closest adult in the field. She looked awful! "Excuse me, ma'am, may I speak with you?"

The ewe turned her head toward Shadow. "I'm not going anywhere. What do you want, dog?" she asked.

"I need to know what has happened here. Why are you in such a mess? Have you heard of foot and mouth?"

The ewe interrupted, "Whoa, whoa, slow down. I'm not feeling too good at the moment, so one question at a time, please. I can answer your questions, but first come around to the other side of me. If the farmer comes into the field, he will see you there."

Shadow moved around the ewe and thanked her for the concern. The ewe continued, "We would normally be moved to our summer pasture before this time, but the farmer has been told he cannot move us from this field. The ministry Menflock come here every day to inspect us for foot and mouth, and we have no food, no shelter, and most of us have foot rot. If we're not moved soon, we will all die."

Rambo asked the ewe if she knew of the white calf, Phoenix.

"I have heard tell of Phoenix, but I don't think she will be able to help us up here. She is down in Devon across the great waters."

Shadow thought for a moment, "How would we get to Devon?"

The ewe laughed. "You can't. It's a long way. You can't walk there. Mind you, there are rumours that some farmers are still moving animals in spite of this stupid rule."

Shadow asked the ewe if she knew of any in the area. "Two farms to the east, I was told they might be up to something. You will have to be very careful."

Shadow thanked the ewe for her time and so wanted to offer her help from this horrible place, but he knew that was impossible. As he had been talking to the ewe, he had slowly got deeper and deeper into the slimy mud. He tugged and pulled, straining as hard as he could. Finally, he began to move.

Rambo was watching him struggle free and thought, *Shadow was right. I would not have got out of that mud.*

It took a little while for Shadow to get free and return to the ditch, but at last, they were together again.

Shadow fell exhausted. He cleaned himself down as best he could. "Just give me a few minutes," he asked.

They rested in the ditch and discussed the ewe's comment about the two farms to the east. Rambo suggested that they should go toward these farms, ask the sheep there if they knew of the illegal movements, and then return to the barn for the night.

"Yes," agreed Shadow, "I think that's a good idea." Shadow was concerned that as yet they had no good news of any description to relay back to the family and was determined to do as much as they could before returning to the barn for the night.

Once again, they were on their way. They didn't look above the ditch again; the sight was too awful. They stayed low and travelled east.

"This water doesn't get any warmer, does it?" said Rambo.

"No, it doesn't, but we can't stop. We have to reach these farms in the next two hours to give us a chance to get back to the barn by dark."

They looked at one another, and both contemplated the possibility of spending the night out in the ditches. They continued forward around fields, through culverts, and over dry stone walls. As they walked, their minds began to wander, nights by the fire for Shadow and warm days in dry fields for Rambo. They could almost feel their respective dreams. Shadow stopped. Rambo bumped into him. "Oh, sorry, Shadow, I wasn't looking."

"Look, I can see two farms and some sheep in the lower valley."

They decided to risk lifting their heads to view the terrain. At a distance of only one hundred metres or so stood a small group of lowland sheep. As they came near, they didn't seem as desperate as the previous group of sheep, but still they were short of food, and upon asking, they knew of the illegal movements thereabouts. "Yes," said the leader of the little group, "that farm over there." She pointed toward the neighbouring farm. "He is going to move his sheep down to Devon tomorrow night to his brother's place. They are usually gone by now, but the Menflock have been stopped by their leaders."

"That's it, then, Rambo. We should get back to the barn for the night and think about what we're to do."

They trudged along the muddy ditches and back to the comfort of the barn. There, they would wait for Pippa to arrive the next morning and inform the others of their intention to go to Devon in search of Phoenix.

When they eventually reached the barn, they were exhausted. They could barely clamber up into the safety of the higher reaches of the haystack before falling asleep. Pippa's new friend in the barn saw them arrive but had not yet been formally introduced, so she thought it best to let them be. *Pippa would be here in the morning; we could talk then,* she thought.

The exhausted pair slept well and deeply. They were warm and dry at last, well, for a while anyway.

Chapter 8
Danger in the Forest

Tom and the others were settling down in the forest for yet another night. Pippa was about to leave to travel south. "Any news for me to take back to the wanderers?"

"Yes, let them know we have decided to take you up on your kind offer of a temporary home in your barn, if that is still okay by you, and tell them that we're all fine. No more frights yet, but the grass tastes horrible; that's why we're moving."

Pippa was very pleased that they would be coming to stay for a while and said, "Great, I will tell them. I will return here two mornings from now, and we will leave early."

The little bat fluttered her wings and started her journey toward Shadow and Rambo, who were fast asleep in the barn. It was a pleasant night, lots of bugs to eat. The damp weather seemed to treble the number of little flying snacks, so Pippa was able to fly almost straight, well, as straight as you will ever see a bat fly, anyway.

Tom, as usual, was standing alert to his surroundings, hoping that the difficulties of the day would stop and allow them all to rest. He had an awful burden over him, looking after his little family, and was not at all sure he was capable of fighting the Menflock.

They seemed so determined to destroy all that mattered to him.

The woodland indeed provided good cover, water, and that horrid grass to eat for the little refugees, but Tom still felt uneasy and was waiting apprehensively for Pippa to return, so she could take them all deep into the forest. As the evening wore on, Tom began to relax. After all, the Menflock never came at night. It was safe to rest. Slight, Gwen, and the twins were warm and dry, and both twins were snuggled into Mother's long, soft wool. Tom decided that he would be more useful tomorrow if he slept while they were safe in the woodland, so he finally nodded his head and fell asleep. The trees lay their thick blanket over them, and a gentle breeze high above them flicked the tips of the trees this way and that as though waving "hello" at the moon.

The forest was home to some strange smells and sounds, the like of which they had never experienced. As the blackness of the night gave way to a glimmer of grey, followed shortly by the first beam of colour, a very peculiar sound rode by, seemingly being carried on the gentlest breeze. Little Hailwen's ears twitched. After a few minutes, once again the strange sound tickled her ears. She opened just one eye. She wondered if she had heard something. After a yawn, she slapped her lips together, and after removing Bethan's foot from her other eye, she rolled onto her back and began to drift off back into a deep sleep. Once again, the faintest sound drifted through the camp. This time, she was sure she heard something, so faint, so far away. She rolled onto her side and raised her head. With her ears pricked up, she listened intently for the strange sound. She looked around but couldn't see anything except trees. She could smell the sweet smells of damp grass, pine needles, and yes, "sniff, sniff," something else, but what was it? She had never smelled anything so sweet. "Mmmmmm, that smells lovely!" She rose to her feet and looked around. All the others were asleep, totally unaware of this strange atmosphere. "Huh, there it is again." She turned her head this way and that to ascertain its direction. When she looked around, she spotted a narrow track, "I never saw that last night. I would have surely gone down there to explore." Once again, the strange but lovely sound drifted into their little camp as though floating on the wind. She looked at her family, thinking better of waking them, yet overwhelmed with her usual curiosity, she looked longingly at the track. "I wonder what it is? I wonder where it goes? What is that smell?" Questions, questions.

With a final look back at her family, she stretched her little legs, gave a yawn, and after a shiver, walked toward the path. As she entered the track, she felt warm and safe. It was so enticing. She thought if she made a noise she would disturb the others, so she crept as quietly as she could along the track. Every now and then, she stopped and held her breath to listen out for the wonderful sound but couldn't hear it. The smell, though, was getting stronger. "This surely is the right way. That smell, oh, that wonderful smell." On she went, deeper and deeper into the forest. She stopped to listen, turning her head she looked back to the track she had walked along, but there was no track, no hoof prints, no disturbed twigs, not even any broken blades of grass where she had just walked. At this point, she should have been very worried, but she was not. "Huh, oh well." Strange senses seemed to be holding her. "I must go on. I must go on." She stopped for a moment but could hear nothing. The smell was still there, but it seemed to be all around her. As she slowly turned her head, she felt a slight breeze. "Ah-ha, that's it. If that sound is having a ride on the breeze, I will keep the breeze in my face, and I am sure to find it." Clever lamb, hey?

She had no idea how long she had been gone. All thoughts seemed to be permeated by the seeming need to go farther. As she continued, a strange light appeared. Still some distance away, she continued with eagerness. The light was all colours: purple, pink, yellow, orange. "Wow, it's so beautiful." Eventually, she came to a clearing in the forest. She stopped at the edge of the tree line to look upon a wonderful meadow. Louder than at any previous time, the sound could be heard, only this time it was clear. "Singing, singing, I can hear it clearly now."

She looked over the clearing in order to find the source of this wonderful sound. In the middle of the clearing, there seemed to be a hollow in the earth. What on earth could make such wonderful sounds? What could make all those wonderful colours? The grass in the clearing looked rich, and oh, it tasted so good. As she moved forward, the grass became even sweeter.

She had to move forward. A raised mound around the perimeter of the hollow in the ground obscured her view. "I just have to go and look inside." She crept forward for what seemed like an age. Eventually, she came to within clear view of the area, yet she still couldn't look down into the hollow. The lights were shooting from within the hollow into the air in every direction. The sound that she had followed was singing, lots and lots of very faint voices singing as loudly as they could and yet still barely audible. It was wonderful. As she approached, she could see flowers, a circle of flowers around the edge of the hollow. She approached carefully, not wanting to frighten whoever could be singing. Slowly, she put her head over the circle of flowers and felt a warm sense drawing her yet forward. "I'll just have a look, just a little look." She edged still closer. She thought that if she at least found out what all of this is about, her mother might not ground her forever when she returned.

She didn't return.

On the morning of Hailwen's disappearance, Tom had woken first. He stood straight and looked at his surroundings. Not noticing at first that one of them was missing, he walked a few feet and turned back to the still sleeping huddle of sheep. The blood froze in his heart. "Hailwen," he shouted, "Hailwen!"

The panic in his voice woke all the others abruptly. "Tom," enquired Gwen, "what's the matter? Where's Hailwen?"

"I don't know. I cannot find her."

They called and looked for the little lamb the whole day but couldn't even find a hoof print, broken twig, or wool snagged on a tree trunk anywhere. She had just simply vanished.

Later that evening, Pippa flew into camp. Tom was standing, looking vacantly into the forest, while Gwen tried to be strong for Bethan, who was weeping silently in the corner, looking into the trees with red eyes and an aching heart. "Will Hailwen be back soon, Mother? Where could she have gone?"

"I don't know, my little one. We won't give up looking for her; don't you worry."

Pippa remained quiet for a few moments, wondering what could have happened. She flew over to Tom, who explained to her that Hailwen had vanished during the night. "Oh, Pippa, my family is getting smaller every day, and I cannot seem to stop it from happening."

Pippa was aware of creatures disappearing in the forest before but was not sure whether to tell Tom what may have happened. Looking at the little group, she decided to tell him. "Tom, listen to me. I have to tell you something. Tom! Tom! Are you listening?"

"Huh, what? Erm, yes, I am listening."

"We have heard tales of mystery in these forests, tales of woodland creatures that are wonderful to behold, tales of creatures that draw you to their hideaways, then they vanish. But the tales all say that the taken ones return after a wonderful time dancing and singing in fairy circles."

"When? When do they return, Pippa? When?"

Pippa thought back to her youth, sitting in small groups listening to tales told of the forest dwellers. "Well, not for some time, in fact maybe not for a long time, maybe hundreds of years."

Tom felt a great numbness wave over him. How was he ever to find his little one? He turned to Gwen. She looked at him. It was in his eyes. She knew her Hailwen would not return. She turned to Bethan, pulling her toward her, and lay in a bed of pine needles.

Tom looked to Pippa, "I am in need of some good news right now, Pippa. What of Shadow and my son Rambo?"

She told Tom that they were fine and that they should have some news shortly. She also said that they should not worry about them but to stay safe.

Tom said to Pippa, "Is it safe to go to your home? I have lost enough of my family. I don't want to lose any more."

"Yes, it's safe! I promise," replied Pippa.

"Then tomorrow we will go with you to your home."

They had looked for little Hailwen all day and the following night and were exhausted. They didn't want to sleep. They felt that if they did, it would signal that they had given up hope of finding Hailwen, but finally, one by one, they reluctantly closed their eyes. Pippa too had been flying all night and needed to sleep, so she looked at her sad, little group, fluttered her wings, and drifted off to sleep.

The exhausted little family slept that day hidden by the trees, protected! Strangely, they were protected by the same forest that had stolen away little Hailwen.

Chapter 9
A Strange Encounter

RAMBO woke with a start. There was something moving on the barn floor below. Shadow was still asleep, so he very slowly crawled over to his position and, in a flash, stuck his woolly leg straight across his face. Shadow awoke, startled by the woolly gag over his mouth.

"Shhhh." Rambo was in front of him with his other front leg in front of his mouth. "Shhhh, don't move. There is something or someone moving down on the floor of the barn."

Shadow's eyes moved left and right, and he nodded to Rambo. Rambo removed his leg from Shadow's mouth. "You ever thought of washing them legs? They taste like rotten wood," Shadow whispered.

Rambo smiled, and they both slowly moved toward the edge of the haystack to look beneath. They gingerly peered over the edge. They could see the floor but couldn't see what was making the noise. There it was again, shuffle, shuffle, snort, snort. Shadow smiled. "Hello, Mr. Badger."

Startled by the voice, the badger said, "Who said that?" The badger spun around on the dusty floor. "Come on out. I've got big, strong teeth, you know. Where are you?"

Shadow put his head over the edge in plain view of the badger.

"Oh, there you are. You can kill a badger like that you know. Frighten me to death, you could."

"I am sorry," said Shadow. "I didn't do it on purpose. You gave us a bit of a start too, you know."

"Us, you said. Who is us? And just how many of you, us, are there up there?" enquired the badger.

"Just the two of us. I am called Shadow, and my friend here is named Rambo."

Rambo looked over to be seen by the badger.

"Well, there is a strange combination, a sheepdog and a ram."

Rambo looked at this strange creature, little legs, round body, and a large, striped head, and yes, very, very big teeth.

"Is he dangerous?" whispered Rambo.

"Only if you are an earthworm."

Shadow climbed down to the floor. "And what would your name be?"

"I am called Brock, yes. Brock, that's my name."

"Well, Brock, we're glad to make your acquaintance."

"Hmm, you too, I suppose, only what are you doing here?" he asked.

Rambo slowly plucked up the courage to climb down to join in this strange encounter. "We're hiding from the Menflock. They are killing all the animals."

"Oh, is that all. That's nothing new to us badgers. We used to be eaten by the Menflock. Now they just hunt us with dogs for fun, and rip us apart, or swipe us with spades, smashing our heads in. The Menflock have even got others trained to track us to our homes and tempt us out with peanuts and syrup. Mmmmm, I love peanuts and syrup." He drifted for a moment as waves of pleasure washed over him, thinking about the treat. Licking his lips, he continued, "Then they lure us into traps and shoot us in the head."

"Yes, I know," responded Shadow. "I met some of the Badger

Boys on the farm where I lived."

Brock looked at Shadow, still trying to understand what all the fuss was about. "You'll get used to it," the badger said, still snuffling about on the floor. "I have."

Rambo and Shadow looked at one another. How could anyone ever get used to a life like that?

"Well, it's been different to meet you. I am going home to bed." The badger shuffled off in the direction of the wall. They watched as he walked straight into it. One of the boards swung forward and returned to its place with a bang. In a swirling cloud of dust, he was gone. They both stood in silence for a few moments, not sure what to make of this encounter.

The sun was almost awake and would soon be up, not that it was going to make much difference today. The clouds were a thick, dark grey and obviously heavy with rain. Shadow and Rambo both wondered if it was worth going farther south. Why not just go back to the forest and wait for all this trouble to subside? Nice thought, but they now knew they had to go south, far south, to Devon!

No sooner had the badger left them than Pippa appeared at the eaves. She looked a little tired, but the journey was not as hard as the previous night. She flew close to them and, as she did, hung onto a wall near to them to give her news.

"Thank you, Pippa, it's good to know they are still safe."

Pippa looked at them both. "Wait, there is more. I need to tell you something."

They both fell silent while Pippa told them of Hailwen's disappearance. A deep pain within them both told of their grief over the loss of such a wonderful little lamb. "When we return, we will find her, won't we, Shadow?"

Shadow looked at Rambo. He also had heard the tales of the forest. "We will at that, my friend, we will at that!"

"I think I can remember how to get there when we return."

"Return? Return from where?" Pippa asked.

Shadow explained what had happened and told her to inform the others that on no account were they to travel anywhere; it was just too dangerous. They told her that they would go south and find Phoenix; she would know what to do. They talked until the sun was high. Pippa had told them that she would not be able to reach them any farther south and said she would introduce them to her friend, who was hanging upside down from the roof. Pippa flew up into the roof space and vanished for a while. When she returned, she said, "This is Mini. She has agreed to pick up my messages from here and continue south to relay them to you."

Shadow turned to Mini, "It's good to meet you. Thank you for your help."

Mini smiled. Then the bats retired to sleep alongside each other high on the gable wall above.

Shadow and Rambo decided to spend that day and the following night resting in the warm barn with plenty of food. They would not be coming back this way for a long time. They would be on their way to the farm in the valley to begin their search for Phoenix.

Chapter 10
Back Up North

Tom and the rest of the family waited patiently for Pippa to return with news of Shadow and Rambo.

"What on earth could have happened to her? It has been daylight for hours." Tom was understandably worried. He didn't want to stay in the area any more than they had to. "Oh, I hope the woodland creatures have not taken her also."

In an instant, Pippa appeared. She looked exhausted. "Sorry I am late, my friends. I had a very difficult trip." She had become disoriented whilst flying. "I was making good time when a sweet-smelling smoke overwhelmed me. I tried to carry on, but I just couldn't sense where I was; there was nothing to see. It just got hotter and hotter when, *bang!* Look." She pointed to her head. "I crashed into a tree, look at the size of that bump! Anyway, there I was, dazed, hanging onto the tree by one leg. After a little while, the wafts of smoke began to clear. Strange colours, strange sounds, and terrible heat. Below me, all I could see was thick smoke, but every few minutes, there was a gap, a long line of dead animals reaching far into the distance. Burning, legs in the air, it was awful. We have to get you to my home as quickly as possible. It was as if the whole world were burning."

Pippa's description of the event she had witnessed sent a great fear through Tom. He looked at the others sleeping. "I thought this couldn't get any worse. I was wrong! Pippa, thank you for being such a valuable friend. Please explain to me again how to get to your barn. As soon as they are awake, I am taking my family out of here."

"Yes, Tom, the quicker, the better, I think." She carefully gave Tom directions to her home. "It'll take a couple of hours at least. I need to sleep now, but I will follow you later to make sure you get there okay." With that, she flew to a nearby tree, hanging onto the trunk, wrapping her wings around her little body as though trying to hide from the horror she had witnessed. Her little wings quivered as she finally fell asleep.

Tom sat thinking for what seemed an age.

"Tom, Tom, are you okay?" Gwen saw him staring into space.

"Yes, I am fine. Get the little ones." He didn't finish. "Get Bethan ready to move, we're leaving this place."

After a short while, they stood in silence, all facing the same direction and looking into the forest, wondering about little Hailwen.

"Father, do you think she is okay?"

Tom felt so desperately sick at the description given to him by Pippa. "Oh, I am sure she is. Hey, we're going to Pippa's place now. Maybe we will find her there. We better move now, or we may miss her." Tom felt that unless hope of finding little Hailwen lay in the direction of Pippa's home, they would never move at all. He knew they had to move.

"Tom, Gwen, I must speak." Slight stood in front of them, barring their way. "I am not going with you. Shush, Tom! Before you say anything, let me finish. I thank you with all my heart for your support, but I have to go back. I have family in the north. I don't know if they are alive or dead, but I must go to them. My partner is gone, I know, but the others, well, I don't know if they are safe or not. I have to go and look for them."

Tom and Gwen fell silent. They looked at her not knowing what to say. Slight continued, "Anyway, we have no idea which way Hailwen went. I just may find her also. If I do, I promise I will care for her until we're all together once more." After a few moments' silence, they all said good-bye and stood in silence as Slight wandered alone toward the pile of stones and back toward Home Hill.

"Take care, my friend, oh, please take care," whispered Gwen.

Slight was never to be seen again! What became of her, we dare not imagine.

"And then there were three," said Tom. "Are you ready, everyone?"

Tom, Gwen, and little Bethan began the long trip deep into the forest toward Pippa's home and safety, they hoped! As they went deeper into the forest, it became darker and darker. "Are you sure this is the way, Tom?" enquired Gwen.

"Yes, my love, I am. Pippa gave a very detailed route to follow. Look, see that gap in the trees? That was caused by a great storm this winter, and some trees fell. Some of them hung up and are leaning, pointing in the direction we should go now."

Gwen felt reassured and knew they were indeed in good hands.

"Come along, we will be there before you know it. Can't be far now, my love."

Together, they continued deep into the forest. After what seemed like an age, a glimmer of light shone between the tall trunks of the trees. They looked at one another and smiled. They knew the forest had given them protection, but it would be so good to see the sky once more. "Just a little more, just a little more." As Tom said these words, he couldn't help wonder what lay ahead. As they approached the forest edge, they crouched low. Peering into the clearing, they could see a large barn.

"Look, Tom, it's huge."

It was indeed. The barn was covered in ivy vines. Up at the top, a section of the roof could still be seen.

Whooshh. "Hi guys, you made good time." It was Pippa. She flew this way and that, shouting, "I know it looks bit tatty, but you wait; it's lovely inside." She flew erratically in the direction of the barn. Tom was very apprehensive about going out into the open in case they were spotted and decided to follow the edge of the tree line until they were closer to the barn.

After a short while, they were just a few metres from the barn. Tom turned to Gwen, "Just wait here for a little while. I will go around the barn to find a way inside."

Gwen carefully took a few steps back into the woodland and tucked little Bethan into her thick, woolly coat. After a careful scan of the area, Tom stepped out into the clearing and took the few steps to reach the barn wall. The vines were thick and seemed almost impregnable. On he went in search of a way into the safety of the barn. After going along all four sides of the barn, he was beginning to worry that they would not be able to get inside. Pippa flew to his side. Hanging on a vine, she said, "Sorry, Tom, I've never had to find a door before. I just fly in, you see. Not to worry, follow me."

Tom followed Pippa around the wall.

"Here we go."

Tom looked. "Look at what? I can't see an opening."

"Exactly," cried Pippa. "That's why it's such a good hiding place. Just move those vines there with your horns." Pippa smiled as Tom hooked his horn under the vine and pulled it back to reveal a single board swinging free. "There you go; told you. I will get the others." Pippa flew around the corner where Gwen and Bethan were hidden. Tom waited for them to appear. "Yes, this is okay. We should be safe here." For the first time, he felt he might be able to protect what was left of his family.

Gwen appeared with Bethan at her side. "Just push this board, my love. It should lift to let us inside."

Gwen gently pushed the loose board. There was a loud creak as the rusty nails were twisted. The board pivoted upward and inward. Gwen stopped. "Come along, Bethan, in here." She looked hesitantly. "Come on, don't worry; I am coming in with you."

Once they were inside, Tom followed. Inside the barn, bright shafts of light shone as the sun found every little crack in the walls and a few in the roof.

"Well, what do you think?" asked Pippa, smiling.

"This is wonderful," said Gwen.

It was warm and mostly dry with a few discarded hay bales to one end.

"Yes, indeed." Tom looked up to the rooftop. "Thank you, Pippa."

"You're most welcome, my friends. I will leave you to settle in. See you later."

Tom, Gwen, and little Bethan sat for a moment.

Now what? thought Tom. It all seemed a bit of an anticlimax, but he knew his role was to conceal his family. He sat and pondered over the plight of the rest of his family in the south and wondered if they were even still alive.

After a good night's sleep, they all felt a little better. Tom stood in the middle of the barn, turning this way and that. "Where on earth?" It was his intention to go outside and have a look around, but where was the door?

Gwen looked on, wondering whether to tell him. "Oh, my big fella. I love you, you plonker," she whispered to herself.

Tom looked at one board. "There you are!" He walked over to the wall, placed his head against the board, and pushed. It didn't move. "Huh." He tried again. "Hmmm, tricky little sucker, hey." He wondered if he were being watched, so he tried not to turn his head. With a deep breath, he walked backward about twenty paces. "I'll show you, ya stubborn thing." His head dropped, and he let fly.

Gwen looked in disbelief. "Tom, *no!* Tom," but it was too late. He was on his way out.

Bang! A cloud of dust wafted in the air. Pippa woke with such a shock. "What's that? What's going on?" Flying to and fro, she flew to Gwen. "What on earth was that? Where is Tom?"

Gwen turned to Pippa. "He's in that dust somewhere. I think he just made a new door."

They both stared into the dust cloud that swirled around, seemingly unwilling to settle. As the cloud thinned, they still couldn't see Tom. As the dust finally settled, they looked but could see him nowhere. "Maybe he succeeded," said Pippa. They looked at one another. "We better go have a look outside."

Gwen walked over to the door they used on arrival and, with ease, lifted the board and went outside. As it was on the opposite side of the unfolding drama, she followed the wall around until she located Tom.

Pippa was clinging to the barn wall. "Over here, Gwen. Come look at this." It was indeed a sight. Tom had entered the outside world with such force that the continued momentum took him for another ten metres or so before finally jamming his head into a hollow of an old oak tree.

It took some time to release Tom's head from the hollow in the tree, but once freed, he said, "I was just, erm, just, erm …" Looking at his situation, he couldn't dream up any story to justify what happened, and so he shook himself off and tried to whistle a few notes as he walked away. "Thank you," he said as he turned the corner. The others just chuckled but not until he was out of sight. Once all were back in the barn, Pippa began to expand on the events of the previous night.

"I am not at all sure of where this took place. As I said, I was completely lost, but I will never forget what I saw. After I regained my senses, I looked into the smoke. It was terrible. There were bodies, many bodies. I had to look closer. As I flew lower, my eyes were streaming with tears, not really sure if it was the horror of what I saw or the smoke. A plume of smoke spread across the ground to the west of the fire, clinging to everything it touched. I flew along the east side to stay out of the smoke. As I was travelling along the side of the never-ending line of dead, burning bodies, I could see sheep, cows, and pigs. It was awful!"

Tom's blood ran cold. "Oh, I hope Rambo and Shadow are safe."

"So far, so good. Don't worry. I have also introduced them to a new friend of mine who will try to keep in touch with them and let us know what is happening. So far, I can tell you they are safe and have decided to cross the great waters to the south. You should stay here for now."

They looked at one another, not sure what to say, but inside the barn was indeed a good place to be. Tom and Gwen got busy making the place agreeable, and Tom pushed a bale of hay to the south wall, where there was a small hole he could use as a spy hole to see the meadow outside. Dusk finally arrived, and Pippa was to start her long journey south to locate Shadow and Rambo. "Well, here we go again. Any messages?"

"Yes, please, Pip. Could you just let them know where we're, please? Wish them well for us."

"No problem," replied Pippa. "See you tomorrow." With a tiny flutter, she was gone.

Tom had one last look through the little spy hole in the wall and returned to Gwen's side. They rested side by side with little Bethan safe between them.

"Good night, Mother. Good night, Father."

"Good night, little one." They lay there, heads together, and allowed the day to leave them.

Chapter 11

Two Go South

AFTER a restful day, plenty of food, and a good night's sleep, Shadow and Rambo left the safety of the warm barn to venture into the unknown and headed for the farm. They knew that the farmer was about to move some of his sheep to his brother's place in the south beyond the great water into Devon. Then they would try to find Phoenix. It was a long way to go, and the farmer knew that the police, army, and ministry officials, including the Badger Boys, would be patrolling, looking out for illegal movements of any animals or of food to feed stranded animals. It was illegal to move anything. If they were captured on the journey, the farmer would be in a great deal of trouble, but the sheep would most certainly be killed. Rambo and Shadow were getting used to the threat of being captured. Maybe Mr. Badger was right after all; you can really get used to living in fear. It seemed such a long time since they left the apparent security of the hill back home.

It was almost dark when they set off. It took a while for them to get safely to the farm gate. They crouched down low to avoid being spotted, and sneaked into the farmyard. Eventually, they stopped about a hundred metres away from a small stock trailer parked in the big open yard. It had been hitched up to a large vehicle. The engine was running. They could hear sheep in the distance bleating as the farmer led them down from the field toward the yard. The area was well lit, but the powerful spotlights were not very well positioned. They provided lots of very dark shadows in the yard. They crept from shadow to shadow to get a little closer to the trailer. Rambo's black fleece was a blessing; he couldn't even see himself.

The atmosphere was very tense. They had to get the timing just right, or they risked being spotted by the farmer when they tried to get into the trailer. They had to get into the trailer after the sheep but before the farmer closed the gate. They just hoped that, in all the commotion, they would not be noticed. Not a bad plan for a sheepdog and a ram, hey? The farmer's wife was parked at the end of the lane, keeping a lookout for headlights of any vehicles. Her job was to warn the farmer of any risks of being spotted.

Rambo and Shadow looked at one another and wondered if they were doing the right thing. Questions raced through their minds: Will they ever be able to return? What will happen to the others when they are gone? Indeed, what will happen to *them?* They were agonising moments, and they were anxious to get moving. Shadow's back legs were shaking like springs about to let go of their tension. "I hate this bit," he said.

"I know what you mean. We will feel better when we get on that trailer. Shh, they're coming back. Look, I can see them," said Rambo.

"Yes, I can see them. You pick your moment. I will move at your pace. There is less risk of spotting one movement than two."

"Okay," agreed Rambo.

The sheep were now coming into the yard. The trailer was a mere twenty, maybe twenty-five, metres away.

"Steady, steady," Rambo mumbled to himself. All but three of the sheep had gone into the trailer, and these had turned back into the field. The farmer turned his back and moved toward the field once more. "This is it. As soon as he goes through that gate, we're moving," said Rambo.

"Go," he whispered as he flew out of the shadows toward the trailer. Shadow was right by his side. Fifteen metres to go. Ten metres. "Nearly there, nearly," whispered Rambo. His heart was pounding so hard.

The farmer was returning. They had to get there quickly. Suddenly, there was a ferocious and angry growl from a nearby shadow, and a sheepdog leapt forward into their path. Shadow instantly turned to defend them, and a vicious fight began. Rambo couldn't stop that quickly if he wanted to and hit the corner of the trailer so hard that he went spinning through the air, hitting about six of the sheep as he crashed into the side of the inside of the trailer.

"For goodness sake," said an old ewe, "what do you think you are doing? I—"

"Stop, now," said Rambo.

The old ewe stood bolt upright but was not going to tangle with such a strong young ram. He was definitely in charge.

"I will explain later, but for now, be quiet."

The fight outside was in full flight. There was hair being ripped out, yelps, and spinning all over the yard, tumbling over and over. Flashes of white teeth slashed aggressively in the dark. Rambo was completely helpless, so he just waited to see the outcome of the fight.

The farmer, of course, heard all the noise and came running back into the yard. When he saw what was going on, he ran into the house, returning with a loaded shotgun. He raised his shotgun and took aim, but the two dogs were in a fierce battle, and neither was showing any sign of giving up. The farmer shouted at the top of his gruff voice, "Willow, Willow, come here girl."

Girl! thought Shadow and released his grip.

Willow ran to the farmer's side.

"I'm sorry," said Shadow. "I didn't know." Once again, the farmer raised his shotgun. Shadow looked at the two big, black holes at the nasty end of the gun and closed his eyes.

"Say good-bye, you filthy mutt," said the farmer. Two sharp clicks told Shadow that both barrels were cocked and ready to fire.

With his finger on the trigger, the farmer slightly closed one eye. Thud! A sharp pain took both legs of the farmer from under him, and the first shot took out the weather vane on the top of the farmhouse. Squeak, squeak, squeak, around and around and around it went. The farmer still didn't know what had hit him, but it had laid him flat. Shadow opened one eye to see Rambo grinning and rubbing his little horns with delight.

"You damned dog," the farmer shouted and started to get to his feet. "I'll have you with the next one."

Shadow thought it best to leave. He turned and fled into the darkness. "Sorry, Willow," he called back. He couldn't help noticing what a beautiful sheepdog she was, with a vivid, reddish-brown coat and a large, white patch on her chest. *Wow, she's very nice,* he thought, as he fled into the darkness.

The farmer lowered his gun and looked up at his weather vane. It had stopped spinning but was full of little holes. It looked funny with the moon shining behind it, and he laughed. "Might need a new one of those, hey, Willow?" he said. He returned to the field to collect his remaining sheep, and after putting them into the trailer, he swung the two wooden side gates over. "Flippin' dog, my leg dun arf hurt." With the trailer gates closed, he gripped the ramp gate.

Oh, no, thought Rambo. He was alone, and as the farmer raised the bottom, hinged tailgate and slammed it shut, he wondered if it were possible for Shadow to get into the trailer or, indeed, for himself to get out. He would be going alone. He felt numb at the thought and looked at the narrow slit at the top of the rear of the trailer. Could even Shadow get up to that small opening? Could he? Rambo didn't think so.

Shadow was outside weighing up his options. *It's not over yet,* he thought. With a loud roar, the engine of the farmer's vehicle burst into life. The vibration was tremendous in the trailer, and this made Rambo feel even more alone. Shadow had to get in, but how?

Shadow walked alongside the trailer. Click, click. Rambo would recognise that sound anywhere. It was Shadow clicking as he did earlier at the big red pen.

"Shadow, Shadow, what am I to do?" Rambo was getting very scared.

"Don't worry, I'll think of a way to get in," he said. *Or on,* he thought.

As the vehicle travelled along the lane toward where the farmer's wife was waiting, Shadow noticed that the stone hedge along the side of the lane was getting higher, and there was one of those red boxes at the end of the lane that Menflock go in to talk to themselves. *Yes,* he thought, *if I time it right, if I just time it right.*

The vehicle was picking up speed as he ran alongside, getting higher as the wall gradually rose alongside the trailer. The red box was getting closer. If only he could jump from the top of the red box and in through the narrow gap at the top of the tailgate. With all his speed and strength, he leapt from the top of the box high into the air. He was airborne. He was almost there, but it dawned upon him that he didn't have enough speed.

Slam! The vehicle came to a very abrupt stop. The farmer had to brake hard because he dropped his lighted cigarette onto his lap. Suddenly, Shadow had more than enough height and far too much speed to reach the trailer and indeed shot through the narrow hole like a shooting star on a clear night. *Bang!* He had passed through the hole and continued toward the front of the trailer, hitting it very hard at the front. He was now hanging with two legs trapped behind the horizontal wooden slats that ran around the inner sides of the trailer.

When the farmer had finished doing the dance of the flaming

trousers, he looked quite satisfied that he may have saved his future offspring from ever existing. Smouldering but undeterred, he got back into the vehicle and continued to drive to the end of the lane. They bumped along the track toward the farmer's wife. "Shadow, oh, Shadow you made it!"

Rambo's spirits were lifted once more. His friend was back, battered, but back.

"Oooh, that hurt," were the only thoughts voiced by Shadow. "Oooh, that hurt so much. Could you get me down, please?" implored Shadow.

The sheep in the trailer were terrified. What did this mad dog want with them? "Not on your life, you crazy dog."

Rambo interrupted them, saying, "Don't be frightened of him. He won't hurt you. We're trying to get south to meet Phoenix. Have you heard of Phoenix?" Rambo asked.

"We have heard some very strange things on the sheep vine," replied one of the ewes, "and now you are expecting us to release a flying dog into this confined trailer?"

"Excuse me," pleaded Shadow. "I might seem a little crazy to you, but there is only one of me and a dozen or more of you, and if you look carefully, you will see I am not exactly in the best of shape here."

"Get him down," said a voice from the corner of the trailer. He can do no harm in here." It was Willow. She too was in the trailer. The sheep huddled together beneath the suspended dog. Rambo climbed onto the back of the group and pushed Shadow upward until finally his legs were free.

"Ohhh, that's so much better. Thank you. My name is Shadow," he continued, "and this is Rambo. We're a recon unit of the W.M.S.F., that is, the Welsh Mountain Special Flock. We're trying to find out about the foot and mouth and to release as many prisoners as we can along the way."

There was silence for a short while. "Put him back," said the old ewe.

"No. No wait," insisted Rambo, "if it were not for my friend here, my whole family would now be dead. The rest of the flock is dead; we saw it happen. He saved us, and we're going to help you." They told the group the tale so far and recommended that the only way they would escape was to make a break for it and form small units as they had done. "You could work in Devon from farm to farm, spreading the news and releasing sheep. We have to go farther south in search of Phoenix. We have to find Phoenix."

Shadow walked over toward Willow. Crouching low, he said, "I am so sorry, Willow. I didn't mean to hurt you." She had two large wounds from the fight, one on her leg, the other on her neck. Shadow crawled on his belly up to injured Willow. Gently, he began to lick her wounds, his ears flat against his head. "I am so sorry, Willow." For the second time, he noticed how she looked. She had beautiful, big, bright hazel eyes and a big, wet nose. Her coat was long, wavy as red as the sunset, and as soft as a puppy's. She was gorgeous! "I must apologise for my appearance. I have had a bit of a difficult time of late," he said, in an effort to explain his mud-covered coat. With a smile designed to impress, Shadow went on to tell her of the events leading up to their traumatic meeting and hoped she would understand his actions.

"So you are doing this to help your friends, the sheep?" she asked.

"Well, yes, they are my family."

She looked at him intently. Tilting her head slightly, she said, "You are very courageous, Shadow."

This was the first time she had spoken his name. It sounded so much more personal coming from her.

Rambo was looking at the couple, watching this relationship unfold before his eyes.

An old ewe nudged him in the ribs. "You're too young to wonder about such things, boyo. You just stay over here with us and tell us more of your adventures. We have never known a sheep to have such a remarkable story, and so young, too."

Rambo turned to the group and felt a lot more secure than he did just a short time ago.

The vehicle slowed. They could see the farmer's wife outside. "Are you sure you want to do this Bob?" she asked.

"No choice, dear. They are not taking my sheep without a fight, and I am not going to watch them die in the mud in the fields."

The comment was heard by the group, and they looked toward Shadow. "We're sorry for not trusting you but—"

Shadow interrupted, "No need to apologise. Just promise to try and escape when you get to Devon."

The farmer gave his wife a hug, and seeing a look of uncertainty in her eyes, he drove off down the lane. After a few miles, they came to a main road. The lights along the roadside flashed through the slits in the side of the trailer. Swish, swish, swish, the wind was disturbed into a deafening roar as they flashed past the lampposts. They were on their way.

All settled down, and Shadow continued to attend to the wounds he had inflicted upon Willow in the farmyard fight. After some considerable time, one of the ewes spoke, "We're almost at the great waters. Look, I can see the floating road." A huge structure emerged in front of them, tall towers and what looked like a floating road disappearing into the mist over the waters.

Rambo became a little worried at this spectacle; it looked eerie and very uninviting. It was hard and cold looking. One of the ewes said, "Don't worry, that will take us to Devon, to safety, and to lovely green grass."

Shadow and Rambo looked at one another. They didn't need to say a word. They hoped that the ewe was right, but they had seen the effect of the ministry's grip and knew they were going into unknown territory. The look said it all.

As they looked around, they could see nothing natural, just a long row of lights eventually disappearing into the mist. No grass, no trees, not even the sky, it was most intimidating. They were travelling very fast, and before long, they were in Gloucestershire, the vehicle headed south for Devon.

So far so good, said the farmer to himself, *just a couple more hours.*

The roads were very quiet. After all, it was well into the night, just the occasional car or overnight delivery wagons trying to avoid traffic jams. The drone of the engine was hypnotic, and time seemed to wander around, not actually getting anywhere.

"Oh, damn, what's that?" The farmer could see a faint, flashing blue light in the distance. It was closing in from behind. *Oh no, oh no, please don't let it be,* he pleaded to himself. Ahead of him was a junction leaving the motorway. Closer and closer, the flashing lights became clearer in his mirror. He decided to get off the motorway at the junction ahead. They might not notice he had a trailer. He swung down the slip road and under the cover of the road crossing overhead. He pulled over and waited for the vehicle to pass overhead. The following vehicle didn't go overhead; it came off at the same junction. "That's it, then; we've had it, sheep. I'm sorry."

He looked desperately at the trailer. With tears in his eyes, he turned to face his pursuers. He knew he was finished.

Around the roundabout, it came straight toward them. Whooosh, it went straight past them with no sign of even slowing down at all. "Ha, haaa," the farmer screamed, "an ambulance! I thought we'd had it for sure then, sheep; for sure I did. Haa, haaa, you idiots." The farmer shouted after the ambulance, "you're supposed to help people, not give them heart attacks." He sat on an old tree stump lying at the side of the road for a few moments to calm himself, and after a short while when his hands had stopped shaking, the farmer returned to his cab. He gave a desperate sigh. With a mighty roar, the engine burst into life, and they were on their way south again.

The passengers inside the trailer were completely oblivious to the events outside. In fact, Shadow was fast asleep curled up close to Willow. Rambo was deep in storytelling. With a captive audience of fellow sheep, he told tales deep into the night. "Whoever heard of a ram doing such things?" they remarked. All stood in awe of this fine, upstanding ram.

The road became very bumpy. They were jostled from side to side. "Guess we have arrived then," said Willow, yawning. On looking down, she saw Shadow still sleeping, lying on her hind leg.

He opened his eyes, and realising where he was lying, he sprang to his feet in a flash. Feeling a little embarrassed, he apologised to Willow, who said nothing but gave him a smile, which told him that she was not offended by his choice of pillow.

Willow turned to Shadow and said, "When we get into the yard, you and Rambo must stay low and in the middle of the group. That way you won't be spotted. We all stay tight; do you hear me, sheep? Are you listening?" The sheep knew better than to argue with Willow; she was a very good sheepdog. "When we get to the field, pick your moment and go. Good luck you two."

On coming close to the farm, the farmer parked the trailer in a dark area of the farmyard. The farmer was still wary of being seen moving the livestock. Once the trailer came to a stop, the little band of sheep huddled tightly together with both Rambo and Shadow squeezed into the middle of the group.

The tailgate of the trailer dropped with an alarming bang. All flinched as their heartbeats raced in anticipation of getting their new friends away safely, so they could continue their quest to search for Phoenix.

"Any trouble then?" called a man as he came out of the farmhouse. He was a tall man with what seemed like no hair at all.

"Hey, Derek. Just bit of a scare is all. I'll tell you all about it over a hot cuppa. Let's get this lot safe first."

The man looked at his brother with a straight face, no smile, no expression whatsoever. "Hmmm, yes, well, safe may be a bit optimistic. Come on, I'll give you a hand." This not-so-encouraging comment was overlooked by the farmer. After such a long drive, he was just glad to be at his brother's farm. After opening the field gate at the end of the yard, they each took hold of the wooden swing gates on each side of the trailer. As they swung them to the side, allowing them to drop into place, they waited for the sheep to blunder out, as sheep do, bewildered and bedraggled. But not one of them appeared to be interested in moving at all.

The two farmers looked at each other and smiled. "Not in a rush, are they?" said Derek.

"Hmm." Bob looked into the trailer. "Willow, you asleep in there, girl? Come, girl, bring 'em on."

Willow looked at the little group huddled to hide the stowaways. "Stay tight, you lot, stay tight." She walked out in front and stood motionless to the side of the gate on the field. With a flick of her head, the sheep walked in perfect unison out of the rear of the trailer.

Bob and Derek looked on as the sheep moved like a rugby scrum toward the gate. "What you been feeding these sheep? Never seen nothing like that, I haven't."

Bob turned to his brother. "Not my doin', don't think. Never done that before, they haven't. Look, even Willow's just lookin' at 'em."

"Well, I reckon that must be the best sheepdog in the entire world," said Derek.

They smiled, and Bob called, "Come on, you lot, you so clever, get in that there field."

Willow once again looked at the little group, saying, "Come on, you lot, get moving."

The farmers laughed as this strange behaviour continued. The sheep moved in a tight group toward the gate and on into the field, eventually disappearing into the darkness. Bob looked at his brother, "Well, I could murder that cuppa now, Deg." After closing the field gate, the two men slowly walked across and into the welcoming glow of the farmhouse for that long-awaited cup of strong tea. Bob turned to Willow, who was still standing in the yard, "Come on, girl." He walked a few metres to a huge barn door and opened a little wicket gate within it. "Come on, girl, get in. I'll bring ya some food when I've had a cuppa."

Willow obediently went into the barn, giving thought to the plight of her new friend Shadow and his travelling companion Rambo.

Back in the field, the little group finally decided it was safe to release Shadow and Rambo. "Well, we did it; you are safe now," said one of the ewes.

"Yes, we are. We thank you all for hiding us so well. How can we ever thank you enough?"

"You just get to Phoenix. Our lives just might depend on it," replied the ewe.

Rambo and Shadow looked at each other. After all, this was a lot of responsibility to handle.

"We will be here on your return. Stay safe," called one of the ewes.

With those words in their ears, Shadow and Rambo ventured into the darkness together. At the field edge, they stopped. "We should follow the hedge around this field. See if there are any local sheep in the fields to ask if they have heard of foot and mouth." With anticipation, they followed the hedge. It was a very large field with little or no drainage ditches in which to hide. The hedge was poorly managed and in desperate need of laying. There were big gaps through which they could be spotted. After a good while, they had not yet seen any sign of sheep or of any other animals. Finally, Shadow turned to Rambo, "I think we should make our way back to the farm. There is nowhere here to give us cover at daylight. We may be in trouble if we rest here only to find we're in the open tomorrow with nowhere to hide and don't know where to go. What do you think, Rambo?"

Thinking a while, Rambo thought back to the comment Shadow had previously made, *Don't confuse cowardice with caution.* Hmmm, yes, that was right. He turned to Shadow, "I agree. Let's go back to the farmyard, see if there is a barn to hide in until morning."

On the return trip to the farm, Shadow noticed a dull patch of what could possibly be a flock of sheep. "Look! Over there. Look. I think I can see ... yes, I am sure there are sheep over there, a few or so fields over."

Rambo looked, squinted, and looked again but could see nothing. Shadow could see him struggling. Shadow knew that the secret to seeing something in the darkness is to look to one side of the target and not directly at it.

"Trust me; there is something there. We need to take a look. They may not be there in the morning."

Rambo agreed and, once they checked their position in relation to the farm, they set off in search of the distant flock. They crossed a number of fields. The night was well along. It was more grey than black, but the sun was still far away beneath the horizon.

Rambo stopped. "Look, yes, over there. I can see a small flock of sheep in that corner by the gate." They made their way over to the flock. They were so pleased, excited even, to see others still free in the fields. Maybe things were okay in the south. As they drew closer, they felt a little uneasy, though neither of them commented on this feeling of something not quite right. They continued toward the small flock. "Maybe they are asleep," said Rambo. Shadow said nothing. They had a great uneasiness about going any closer but knew they had no choice.

As they approached, both stood silent. What they saw hit them in the pit of their stomachs.

Dead sheep! Dozens of murdered sheep. They were lying in a heap in a dirty, muddy corner. Their twisted, contorted bodies were lying as though thrown down with no respect whatsoever. To one side, a small pile of newborn lambs lay in a pool of cold, muddy water, some with broken legs. They were probably crushed to death by the adult sheep panicking to stay alive. Looking at the adults, they noticed each had a hole in the top of their heads. Blood ran from the hole. There was a strange, hissing sound. "What is that sound?" they wondered. Looking again, they noticed that the corpses were swollen, the legs stuck out at unnatural angles due to the bloating. This was indeed the most horrific thing they could have seen. "Oh, Rambo, we have made a terrible mistake. Have we left our family to a fate such as this?"

Rambo looked at him. He had a distant, blank expression on his face.

Shadow was a little disturbed by Rambo's expression.

"No, Shadow, be strong, we won't let the Menflock destroy everything they choose. We will fight to stay alive. This must not continue. This must *stop!*"

This was the moment that the young ram they all knew and loved ceased to exist. "We're not safe here, Shadow. We need to get back to the farmyard before sunup." They looked to the east. "Let's go" Rambo continued; "we don't have much time, my good friend."

They both felt a bond not felt before, a bond only felt by ones experiencing horror side by side. They retraced their steps to the farmyard in complete silence. As they returned to the gate, they had entered after leaving the trailer, they looked across the yard and saw a barn on the opposite side.

The small wicket gate was ajar. "That's our place for the night, come on, Rambo." The yard lights were now off and the house seemed to be quiet and mostly in the dark except for a flicker in a small window overlooking the yard.

They stopped outside the barn door and peered inside. It was dark, dry, and full of bales of hay. On creeping in, they climbed up onto the hay bales, heading for the uppermost part of the barn.

"Boo!"

"Oh, my word, Willow! You almost scared us to death. Why do you always hide in the shadows?"

"Oh, I'm sorry" I like shadows! Rambo turned to his friend and smiled. "I am so glad to see you, but why are you back here? I thought you would be miles away by now."

Rambo quietly climbed up to the top of the barn, leaving Shadow to tell Willow of the terrible find in the field just a short distance away. It was a still, clear night. No rain tonight. Rambo sat silently contemplating the fate that may have already overtaken his family in the north. Looking through a small gap in the sidewall of the barn, Rambo watched the stars, sure he could recognise some of them from Home Hill. Shadow and Willow curled up together in the hay below. Exhausted, but warm and dry, they slept soundly.

"Cock-a-doodle-doooo."

"What on earth was that?" called Rambo.

"Don't worry, Rambo. It's our early morning call. It's a cockerel."

"Well, I don't like it. It's too loud."

Shadow and Willow smiled and called him down from the top of the barn.

"Shhhh." Willow's ears stood upright. "The farmer is out. He's coming over here. Hide, quick, quick, hide."

Rambo stayed where he was, and with a tremendous leap, Shadow sat at his side.

Click ... The latch on the wicket gate rose, and the door swung open. With a piercing squeak, the door fully opened, allowing Bob to enter the barn. "Hey, girl," he called, "good morning, girl. Come on, look what I got for you. Ummmmmmm, fresh meat, biscuits, and a nice cup of tea. You like your cuppa tea, don't you, girl?"

Willow came out of the shadows, crouching low, almost sliding along the floor, all her teeth showing with excitement to see her master.

"Actually, I don't like tea at all, but I drink it because you look so pleased when I do."

Unfortunately, Bob, who didn't speak dog, didn't understand a word, so she just looked at his big, smiling face and began to drink.

"Good girl, you enjoy your breakfast now." He turned away toward the gate. Bump! "Ow, flippin' 'ek. I hate that gate. Thirty years I been banging my head on that flippin' gate!" He closed the latch behind him. In the distance, his brother could be heard laughing. As the voices faded away, the three looked at one another. Willow ran to the door. Peeping through it, she could see the farmer go back into the farmhouse, still rubbing his aching head.

"Hey, guys, pssst, Shadow, Rambo, you can come down now." Down they climbed from their hiding place above. Rambo slipped and landed with a bit of a bump and in a cloud of dust. "No broken bones, all okay," Rambo stated emphatically.

Willow looked to Shadow, "I would like you to eat this meal. I know you have not eaten in days, and you will need your strength to carry this task through."

"No, I couldn't."

"Hey, please eat it. I get two meals a day. Eat it, or you won't be going anywhere."

"Oh, thank you, Willow. I love tea in the morning."

"Well, there you go then, you're doing me a favour. I drink it to please my master. I don't even like it."

Shadow lapped up the sweet tea. "Oh, that is so good."

Willow smiled. She nudged the bowl of food toward him and stepped back. "Eat, my friend, get your strength back. Then you can tell me what you plan to do now you are here."

Shadow was not sure what their plans were from here, but he did know this meal may be his last for a while, so he tucked in and enjoyed every mouthful.

They were all taken by surprise when a loud squeak told them that the wicket gate was opening. In sheer fright, Rambo and Shadow leapt into the rim of a discarded tractor tyre on the floor of the barn behind a large, rusting, old tractor. The farmer, hearing the scuffles, looked at Willow. "Sorry, girl, did I give you a fright then. I see you're nearly done with your food, hey. Come here, girl; I need to look at those cuts on your leg. Oooh, that's nasty. I should have got that damn dog. Don't you worry; if he ever comes back, we'll 'ave 'im. Hey, I shot my weather vane, I did."

Willow looked toward Shadow. "If only you knew what a brave, wonderful dog he is."

The farmer looked at his much-loved dog, saying, "I swear you can talk sometimes, my girl. Wish I could understand you, dog. Come here." The farmer pulled out a spray can from a pouch he was carrying "Hey, you did a good job cleaning these wounds, girl."

Shadow smiled. "That was me," he whispered to Rambo.

Rambo elbowed him, "Shhh."

The spray can was applied to Willow's wounds. A vivid purple spay covered her leg. Pssssssssssst, pssssssssssst.

"That's you sorted, girl. Stop it getting infected, that will."

Willow was not sure whether to lick him or bite him. *If only you knew how much that stuff stings*, she thought.

With a smile and a pat on her head hard enough to knock her brains out—this man had hands like shovels—the farmer then left. Shadow and Rambo came out of their hiding place and stood next to Willow

"Willow, will you please eat the rest of that meal? I feel much better now. Don't want to overdo it. I may have to move fast later."

With a smile, she walked over to the bowl and ate.

"Well, Rambo, it's about time we planned our next move."

For a few moments, they stood silent, not sure what the next move was. After a while, Rambo suggested they try and do a recce on the immediate area. "Look right up there." The sun was sending an ever-widening shaft of light from the eaves of the barn down to the lower reaches of the haystack. The dust in the barn made the shaft of light dance as it swirled around, never seeming to land. They stood for a moment, watching this spectacle.

"Hmmm, well," began Shadow, "if I were to climb up there onto those beams, I could see for a great distance. Then we will know which direction has the most sheep to ask about Phoenix."

"Wow, it's an awful long way up, Shadow," said Willow. "You will have to be very careful."

Willow stood alongside Rambo and watched as Shadow climbed up the hay bales then again higher up onto the high beams that ran the full width and length of the barn. Willow was right; it was an awfully long way up, or was it an awfully long way down; that seemed more important from where Shadow stood. With trepidation, he stepped onto the first beam. It was thick with dust, very fine dust that seemed to fill the air at the slightest touch. "Watch your eyes down there," he called, just in time to see Rambo rubbing his eyes as he stood in a shower of falling debris. "Sorry." Shadow continued gingerly along the beam. The balancing act was made more difficult by the natural wavy edge of the beams. At times, the beam was only a little wider than his paws. As he turned back, he could see a trail of paw prints in the dust. It did cross his mind that this may have been the least sensible of the choices open to them, but as he couldn't imagine what other choices there might be, this was it.

At last, Shadow reached the upper eaves of the barn and peered through to the fields beyond.

"What can you see?" called Rambo. There was no reply. "Shadow," he called again, "how many sheep are there."

"None this side, but we got three more sides yet, so don't worry." Shadow was of course worried. He could see such a long way, miles and miles it seemed, and not one white coat could he see. "I will climb higher." A section of the brickwork gable corbelled out to provide steps just wide enough to get to the higher reaches of the huge roof. "There you go. I'm okay," he called, trying to convince himself.

He spoke too soon. His next step was not so sure. Shadow's rear left leg slid quickly off the wavy edge of the beam. All below gasped in horror as Shadow disappeared from view in a cloud of thick dust. They heard a muffled bump, followed by another as Shadow hit the beams previously ascended. They waited for the inevitable thump. With eyes closed and time ticking by, nothing happened. They both called, "Shadow, are you okay?"

"No problem," he replied in a rather croaky, strained voice.

They dared to look up. As the dust cleared, they could see a silhouette of a dog sort of floating in midair. It didn't look like Shadow; it was a pale grey-looking colour.

"Hi guys! I am fine. Just covered in dust." Shadow was saved only by his thick leather collar, which caught on a hook in the side of the beam below. There he hung, swinging to and fro. "Hmmm," he mused, "how do I get back up onto the beam?" He looked below. "Wow, that's a really long way down." After what seemed like an eternity, he decided to try and swing backward and forward, and when he thought he had enough swing, he would slip out of his collar and land on the hay bales. "Easy." He hoped!

His tail swung first, then his legs, followed by his backside, followed by his body. Higher and higher he went. Eventually, everything was in unison. Clouds of dust followed his motions back and forth, backward, forward. "Nearly there. *Go!*" He slipped his collar, and his body twisted through the air. Plumes of gray and yellow dust spiralled behind him. Would he make it? Of course he did.

"Phew." Shadow sat for a moment, heart pounding, before daring to look over the edge of the bales to his friends below.

"Shadow, are you okay?" called Willow.

"I'm okay. Don't worry." As he looked over the edge of the bales down to the floor, he put on a brave smile and said, "Good collar, that."

They all looked at the collar still hanging from the hook in the beam. He knew he just had a lucky escape from a very nasty fall. He also realised that, as he no longer had the collar on, he couldn't afford another slip such as that one. He bravely climbed high onto the beams again. Looking in all directions from this vantage point, he could still not see any sheep, well, apart from the carcasses of the flock they happened upon the previous night.

After finally coming down to earth, he was again alongside his friends. He told them the bad news, and together, they decided that they should continue as planned and go farther south in search of Phoenix. With full tummies and a purpose in mind, Shadow and Rambo said a final farewell to Willow and headed farther south.

"Good-bye, my friends, please take care. I hope you come back this way when this is all over."

Shadow looked back and smiled. They turned away and were soon gone from view.

Chapter 12
Death of a Thousand Sheep

WEEKS went by, and endless miles seemed to roll along. Sleep didn't come easily these days. Each attempt was broken by moments of fear or worry about the plight of their family so far away. Before the light had turned the colourless night into day, Rambo awoke. They had spent the night in a hollow tree. There was an eerie silence. As Rambo put his head close to the opening in the trunk, he sniffed the cool morning mist. Everything seemed so still.

He turned to one side to see his friend, Shadow, still sleeping, but as he was twitching and whimpering, he was obviously not resting well. He decided to wake him. "Psst, psst, Shadow," he whispered, "you awake, my friend?"

"What! Who said that?"

"Only me, don't worry. Just thought we better make a move before daylight. We may be exposed here. It's a long way to the edge of the field. We have to find a better L.U.P."

"Yes, I agree," said Shadow.

After a few moments to gather their thoughts, they continued on their quest to find Phoenix. As they continued, familiar sounds wafted on the air. A cockerel was crowing. Nothing seemed to have changed in his world. As they continued along the field edge, they were startled by a pheasant that seemed to shoot into the air in an instant. "Excuse me, can we speak?" But the bird was already gone. "Wow, in a bit of a hurry, that one."

"Yes, he was, but I know why!" Shadow turned to Rambo. "That was a pheasant. Did you notice that red flash on his face?"

"Yes, I did. What's his story then?" He just knew this couldn't be good. They stopped for a moment in a small hollow in the ground.

Shadow told Rambo how pheasants are captive birds, reared for the sole purpose of being killed for fun. He explained how they are protected from danger from foxes whilst young only to be released in the woodland.

"That doesn't sound so bad," said Rambo.

"I haven't finished yet! Later, a long line of Menflock called beaters enter the woodland, and using sticks, they push the birds forward through to the woodland edge. Once they are almost out of the wood, a long line of cord, like the bailing twine at the big pen if you remember it—"

"Yes, I remember it. You chewed it off."

"Yes, like that. Well, this twine has bits of something tied to it that flap around, and the pheasants won't step over it. They are trapped! Menflock approach with sticks from behind and with a twine from in front that they won't step over. Only one place left to go, *up!* Just like he did. They take to the air to escape, not knowing that a row of Menflock is eagerly awaiting their desperate attempts to escape." Shadow stopped speaking for a moment. "Sorry Rambo, thought I heard a noise." They carefully raised their heads above the rim of the little hollow but couldn't see anything. They dipped back into the hollow.

"Well," said Rambo impatiently, "tell me."

Shadow continued, "Well, the line of Menflock follow the flying birds with guns as they rise into the air." Shadow explained to Rambo the purpose of a shotgun and its role in this affair. "*Bang,*

bang. Two shots they have, but there may be six or more guns lined up to try and blast their quarry from the sky." They were quiet for a moment until Shadow continued, "But not all are good shots, and some birds escape, such as our friend there."

"Is there no animal safe from the Menflock?"

"Not that I am aware of," replied Shadow.

Rambo looked at his friend. "Why did he fly away from us? We didn't want to harm him!"

"No, we never would, but he is not to know that. Remember that men use dogs for sheep, cows, and all sorts of jobs. Well, they also use dogs to chase pheasants from cover. That poor bird saw me and froze until he couldn't stand it any longer before taking to the air. He was terrified!"

Rambo shook his head but said nothing. What words would make sense of this world? *How could we have been so unaware of the world around our home on the hill?*

"Hey, remember he got away. He has a good chance of staying free and alive. The Menflock do try and catch the ones that get through the guns by tempting them with food in big traps, but the smart ones like our friend there move on."

"Like we have?"

"Yes, I suppose so. Hey, we best be moving on too."

They had more times like this as they worked their way south; because they were tired, weary, and hungry, travel was hard for them. Very carefully, they raised their heads to look around for potential threats, but all seemed quiet for the moment. They continued south, keeping the sun to their left. It was easy to work out because Shadow had a small white patch on his left front paw.

Not too far away, they made out the silhouette of a huge barn. "Now that's worth a look, hey, mate," said Shadow, smiling at Rambo. Each time they had encountered such a place, they had found food and shelter. Slowly, they moved forward, constantly aware that they could be spotted in such a flat, open area. As they grew closer to the barn, they could hear sheep bleating. They knew better than to raise false hopes so continued on without mentioning the sounds coming from the barn. The sides of the barn were of a wooden slat construction. Gaps between each vertical board would allow them to look inside.

"Shadow, down!" cried Rambo. "Get down. Menflock are coming," he was right. Four of them walked together, already dressed in white, holding blue pithing rods and a shiny, captive bolt gun, laughing as though they had not a care in the world. "We need to get out of here, now!" They turned away. Keeping low, they crept away from the barn.

At the corner, Shadow turned to check they had not been seen by the Menflock.

"Wow, now that was close," said Rambo. His heart was pounding. He ran deep into the scrub and dropped to the ground. Realising he was alone, he looked back to the barn. "Shadow, Shadow, where are you?" He scanned the area and saw Shadow hiding under a sheet of corrugated tin. Two men stood very close to him. Rambo dropped back to the ground. "Oh, *no!* Shadow, oh Shadow, oh, please stay still."

It was too late! One of the men stamped hard on top of the metal sheet covering Shadow and, grabbing him by the scruff of the neck, dragged him out, lifting him into the air. "What we got 'ere then? Not one o' my dogs, this ain't." Looking at Shadow, the man said, "Bit tatty, ain't ya, dog?" He opened the door of the barn and threw Shadow inside. Shadow hit the ground hard, finally coming to a stop against an empty water trough. "He can go with the sheep." Without another word, he walked away.

Rambo looked around but could no longer see any Menflock. "I've got to get my friend out of there and quick." He gingerly approached the barn. Inside were six Menflock all set up for work. How many sheep were in the barn Rambo couldn't tell; it looked like every sheep in the world. The noise was deafening!

Rambo was numb. "How on earth do I get him out of there? I can't fight them all!"

As he was wondering how to rescue Shadow, he looked across the carpet of steaming, dirty-looking wool, trying to find him. On the far side of the barn sat Shadow. He looked so frightened. Next to Shadow, two Menflock were working. Bang! Bang! Bang! One by one, the sheep were dropped and, shortly afterward, leant over by another Manflock, and each one was pithed hard until the poor animals finally gave up their hold onto life and died. No wonder he looked so frightened; maybe he was next!

"I have to get him out."

As the hours went by, approximately half the barn was still. A cloud of steam enveloped the upper reaches of the barn. Two of the Menflock stood tall and looked at one another. "Look at the state of you," one of the Menflock said. The man was covered in blood.

"My ears are ringing with all this noise. I need water."

The two Menflock climbed out of the pen they had been working in and walked over to where Shadow was lying motionless, ears down and trembling. After taking a drink, one of them said, "What we gonna do with this 'ere dog, then?"

"Farmer said he would sort it out later. He gonna shoot it, I guess. Shame really, but he don't need it now, do 'e? We killin' all his animals."

"No, guess not."

Shadow could hear this conversation. *Strange how, just because they cannot understand what us animals say, they assume we can't understand them,* thought Shadow. He was listening to every word, wondering what the future held for him.

"Well, Sam, what do you think of the day so far?"

Sam had only that day been assigned to assist in this carnage by his commanders. He was a navy man. "I have seen many things in my career around the world and taken part in three wars. Nothing has prepared me for this killing of innocents. I retire next year. I just wish I had retired last week!" He looked down at his blood-soaked suit, no longer white.

"Hey, it'll soon be over, mate; rumours have it we will be finished soon. Only a few more weeks. I've only had three contaminated farms this week. It's definitely slowing down. We'll all be able to go home, mate. Oh, well, let's get bloody. Hey, mate, few hours' work here yet."

They both looked at the task ahead and began walking back to the pen. Shadow, listening to what had been said, was so pleased that this may soon end but was not convinced he would be alive to see it.

Rambo slowly made his way around the perimeter of the barn, looking for weak points to get his friend out. On the second wall, one of the boards had suffered some damage and was held in place by a single pin at the bottom. Rambo knew this might be the only possibility of escape, so he lay deep and quiet in a nearby nettle bed to consider his options. From his L.U.P., he could see Shadow clearly and was preparing to ram that wall hard to shatter that board and rescue Shadow, well, in theory anyway. But he was not so sure he could smash the board. He might just knock himself senseless, and then he would be in there too. He mumbled to himself. "Don't confuse cowardice with caution. Don't confuse cowardice with caution," he repeated.

"Oh, blow this, enough is enough." His head went down, he felt the power build in his strong frame, and his head shook. With one final look, he let fly. As Rambo hit the barn wall, it did indeed damage the board. In fact, splinters filled the air, and what remained of the board went high into the air. He had built up such a momentum that the strike didn't even slow him down. His momentum carried him flying into the barn. The two Menflock near the exploding wall, startled by this flying ram, looked at one another. Shadow raised his head. Ears straight up, eyes bright and grinning, he waited to see what would happen next when his friend finally came to ground.

The two Menflock, still motionless, looked toward the hole in the wall. Rambo, still travelling very fast, hit one of the men in the back. He felt a number of the man's ribs crack with the impact. The other man stood with his hands on his hips, looking at his injured partner. He took one step forward, oh, but what a step! He leaned toward his injured mate lying on the floor just in time for the remnant of the flying board to return to earth. It hit him square on the back of his head. "Ow!" He crouched down, rubbing his newly acquired bump.

He won't be chasing us today, he thought. "Shadow, get up; get up now!"

Shadow finally sprang into action, and in the blink of an eye, they were gone. By the time the Manflock still standing stopped rubbing his head and hurled abuse at the other four Menflock at the other end of the barn, who were laughing intensely at these goings-on, they were in deep cover.

The Manflock went to look through the hole, but they couldn't be seen.

Safe again, the two warriors went to ground to recover from the ordeal. "The injured Manflock, I would imagine, went home or wherever they go when they get beaten up by an angry ram, especially a tough, Black Welsh Mountain Ram.

They stayed low for the rest of the day, worried about being spotted, but all was quiet. It seemed that the Menflock didn't even try to come after them. "Well," said Shadow, "that was a close one. Thank you, my friend. To think when we started out that you were worried about being brave enough. You, my friend, are the bravest ram I have ever met. I owe you my life. Your father, Tom, would be so proud of you."

Well, Rambo was so pleased to hear those words that he grinned until the dried mud matted in his wool cracked. "You're welcome, my friend," replied Rambo.

Shadow told Rambo what the Manflock said in the barn.

"Oh, do you think …? What if …? Oh, Shadow."

"Let's just wait and see, hey? We're obviously not safe yet."

They thought it best not to stay in the area and retreated farther into the undergrowth to wait for the safety of darkness. As they sat waiting, Shadow told Rambo of a conversation he had had with one of the captives in the barn. "An old ewe spoke to me in there. She said that Phoenix was not far away, just a few miles. Maybe we will find the answers we need there."

They needed this hope so much. Memories of their lives before this time seemed to be fading away. "Hey, I wonder if Willow is okay," said Shadow.

"Oh, I am sure she is. She is well loved by that Manflock," replied Rambo.

"Yes, she is. Maybe they are not all the same."

Unknown to them, there were indeed many Menflock trying to stop this terrible execution of animals, though they had not seen any evidence of it and were not willing to expose themselves to find out. As darkness fell, they decided to move, driven by the possibility that answers might lie ahead.

"Come on, Rambo, let's do this together."

Chapter 13
Pyres by Night

SHADOW and Rambo travelled in the darkness, and before first light, they took shelter in a small cave in a rocky outcrop. "Should be okay in here, Shadow. Look, there's a back door if we need to run." He was right. It was a very small hole, and not so long ago, neither of them would have gotten through it, but now they were so weak and thin that only fear and determination were spurring them on. Even if this were over tomorrow, would they have the strength ever to reach home? It was unlikely. Without any conversation, they both slept until about midday. A noise in the cave woke them. With hearts pounding, they tried to see what made the sound, but it was too dark. Shadow crouched low to the ground, growling and creeping forward to defend them.

"No need for that. I won't hurt you." In a tiny little crack up in the far reaches of the cave hung a bat. "My name is Sticky. Are your names Shadow and Rambo, by any chance?"

"Well, yes, that's us. How did you know?"

"Oh, my dear fellows, we have been looking for you for ages. We were not sure if you were still alive. Nice to meet you," said the bat with a big upside-down smile.

"Oh, please tell us news, news of our family, news of foot and mouth. Oh, it's been so long."

"Well, you must stay here today. There is a lot going on here, so I will talk for a little while."

"Oh, thank you so much, Sticky."

She began to tell them of Tom, Gwen, and Bethan, all long lost to them in the north. "They are fine. They got safely to the home of, erm, oh dear, *Pip!* Yes, Pip's home, and so far, as reports go, they are still there. Now I have been talking to Phoenix."

"Phoenix!" cried the two. Because of Phoenix, the killing just might stop.

"Well, her and the family of Menflock that she lives with … I will let her tell you the tale herself, but not today."

"Oh, please, Sticky, take us to her now," pleaded Rambo.

"No. Trust me. If I take you now, you will be dead by nightfall," stated Sticky. "I need a few more hours' sleep before I go off to feed, and I will tell my friend to pass the message on that you are well and have found Phoenix. I will return here tomorrow. I will probably not have any news for you from your family, as it is taking thirteen flights to reach your friend Pippa." With that, Sticky crawled deep into the little crack.

"Sticky," called Rambo. "Sorry, Sticky, just one more question. Why do they call you Sticky?" Rambo had not lost his curiosity.

Sticky looked at him and smiled. "On my first flight, I left my mother's side and successfully landed on a nearby tree. Unfortunately, it was a pine tree, and I landed in a big, dripping patch of resin. It took her hours to get me out. See, *Sticky!* Good night!"

"Good night, Sticky." Both Rambo and Shadow smiled.

"Oh, Rambo, could it be true? Are we truly near the end of this horror?" Both of them were secretly hoping but thinking about what she said about a lot going on around here. They wondered what on earth could be going on. They decided to stay in the cave until it was dark before venturing out to see what she meant. They rested that afternoon. Both of them were hungry and restless.

As the sun dropped low in the sky, Sticky reappeared. With a big yawn, she exposed lots of gleaming needle-sharp teeth. "Hello, Sticky." She jumped back into the hole for cover.

"Sorry, Sticky, didn't mean to startle you."

"Wow, I thought I dreamt you two were here."

"No dream. Here we're!"

She ventured out again. Looking at the two, she remembered their conversation earlier in the day. "Well, I'll go now. Long way to go, good news to tell. See you two here in the morning." She fluttered off into the darkness. It was so good to think that they had re-established contact with the rest of the family in the north.

It was now very dark, except that they could see a warm, glowing light hugging the horizon.

"What do you think, Rambo? Worth a look?"

"Yes, it might be a farm. We need to get you some food."

Without further discussion, they ventured into the darkness. Keeping to the field edges, they made their way field by field. "I didn't think this was so far away."

"No, nor did I," replied Rambo. "Can't be far now."

No sooner had he spoken those words than they heard a sharp crack! "Down, get down," whispered Rambo. They lay motionless against a hedge when two legs appeared right in front of them on the other side of the hedge. They froze and waited. Had they been spotted or heard? They hoped not. They could see two Menflock, but what could they be doing here at this late hour? As the Menflock moved away, they seemed to be looking for something, parting the grass with their boots. They were hard to spot in the darkness as neither wore white. In fact, they were well camouflaged.

"Badger Boys," whispered Shadow.

"Do I want to know?" replied Rambo.

"No. We're in trouble. We need to follow them very carefully. We cannot afford to lose them. If we lose them, they will have us."

Rambo nodded. "Okay."

As they moved forward, Shadow parted the grass to expose a shiny, suspended snare.

"What on earth is that?"

"It's a snare. If you get your leg caught in it, you are trapped. When they return, they have got you."

Suddenly, there was a rustling in the bushes ahead. The two Menflock ran forward. "Got ya."

All the commotion allowed them to move a little closer. "It's a fox," stated Rambo. "Why are they catching a fox?"

One of the men smiled and knelt down alongside the struggling fox. He pulled a large knife from his belt.

"Oh, what a relief; it was a mistake, look he's cutting it lose." Rambo relaxed.

The man slid the blade under the snare, and leaning forward, he plunged the blade deeply into head of the fox. "Shh, shh, shh, there you go, all done now." After a few moments, he twisted the knife sharply and sat up onto his knees.

"Now, that's how you do it." Pleased that he had done a good job, he wiped the blood from his metal blade and returned it to his belt.

Rambo was left shaking from this terrible event, and his trembling leg was moving the grass in which they were hiding. The Manflock lurched forward to catch what he thought was another victim for his blade.

"*Go!*" yelled Shadow.

Rambo leapt into the air, accidentally butting the Manflock hard in the face. The man launched upward and backward into the air and, landing flat on his back, lay very still. His mate was just a few metres away and made a desperate grab for Rambo. He was left only with a clenched fist full of black wool. "What the hell was that?" said the injured killer.

"Ha, ha, that was brilliant," said his mate.

Rambo and Shadow fled into the darkness, hoping not to be caught by one of the snares hidden in the undergrowth. Shadow explained to Rambo who the Badger Boys were and said, "They must be trapping animals around the farms." The so-called Badger Boys had indeed been assigned this task. It was thought that the disease might be carried by wild animals as they moved around the countryside. As their usual weapons had been recalled, they were issued with steel bars to smash in the heads of captured animals or were instructed to use their imaginations and find other methods to kill their quarry.

Shadow and Rambo dropped into a deep rut in the ground. Out of breath, they lay back against the vertical side of their hideaway. "Well, here we're again, sitting in a muddy ditch," said Rambo.

"Hmm, yes indeed."

Looking around, Shadow grew curious about this newfound ditch. It was deep, almost a metre, well above their heads. The sides were vertical, and the floor had deep grooves of mud in it. "Tyre tracks!" muttered Shadow. "Tyre tracks, Rambo. This is not a drainage ditch. A very large farm vehicle has been here. We can follow this away from here." The pair followed this deep rut in the mud across two fields and into a third. They stopped for a moment.

"What is that awful smell?" asked Rambo. "And that noise?"

Carefully, they raised their heads to look into the field. It was horrible! In silence, they looked at a wall of intense fire raging. The heat was burning their eyes, but they couldn't turn away. In each direction, the wall of fire followed the lay of the land, dipping lower to their left and rising with the higher ground to the right. Neither Rambo nor Shadow could see to the end of this wall of flame.

As the purpose of this fire dawned upon Shadow, he turned around and slowly slid down the muddy wall, followed shortly afterward by Rambo. "Why would any creature do something like this?" It was a question stricken with anguish. The fire was filled with the dead. It hissed and whined as the swollen and contorted bodies released gasses into the air. Burning calves alongside their dead mothers, lambs thrown on the top, and burning wool left plumes of smoke into the air. They had not smelled the fire before as they were still upwind of this carnage. The smoke could be seen in the sky, rolling away into the valley below. No words could describe the sight.

Bang! Bang! Two sharp cracks sent entrails flying wildly through the air from bodies that could no longer hold the building gasses. Ejected flesh lay in small parcels across the ground. Shadow raised his head with his back to the pyre. The light from the pyre was bright. It dawned upon him that this was the distant light they had seen earlier in the evening. They had hoped it to be a farm. As he looked into the lighted area, he could see two foxes and many rats tearing at this free banquet set out before them. He quietly rejoined Rambo in the mud. "I am sorry, Rambo." He looked at his friend.

"Hey," said Rambo, "don't say that. I am so proud to be here next to you, my friend. We're not beaten yet. Come on, let's move on."

Together, they continued farther along the ruts in the ground following the line of the pyre. They could see an area of woodland ahead, but it was still a fare way to go. They noticed that the noise of the pyre was getting louder. As they looked up, they could see the smoke high in the air. Rambo looked at Shadow. "The wind, the wind is changing direction. The smoke is coming this way." They both knew that they had to get out of there and quickly! The crisscross pattern of the vehicle tracks in the mud ran in every direction. If they were to lose their bearings they would not be able to see the tree line and they would be lost in this place. Easy pickings for the returning Menflock in the morning. The wind had indeed changed direction. The sky could no longer be seen, only the wafting, swirling plume of smoke. A range of colours mixed in amongst the white swirls left steaks of yellows, pinks, purple, and dark grey, all effectively barring their way to the field above them and their escape.

Shadow suddenly stopped.

"What's up?" whispered Rambo.

Shadow turned toward him saying, "There is a Manflock sitting in the ditch. He must have been caught out by the wind like us. We're stuck!"

The Manflock was patrolling the pyre. He had a long stick with a sharp point at one end. It was his job to walk along the length of the pyre, plunging the sharp stick into the swelling bodies of burning animals to release the gasses, thereby reducing the number of free meals being flung into the air for wild animals to eat.

"What are we going to do?" asked Rambo.

"We can't do anything. We're stuck here for the moment. Let's just hope the wind changes direction again." Shadow sat in a position where he could keep an eye on the Manflock ahead just in case he decided to crawl in their direction. Soon, the smoke was hugging the ground so tightly that it occasionally wafted down into their muddy trench. "Wow, I hope that stays up there," said Shadow. He looked along the trench to see the Manflock ducking as low as he could to escape the acrid smoke. Their coats were covered with a thick film of grease from the burning bodies, and the smell was so strong, sweet yet sulphurous and inescapable.

Turning his head slightly, Rambo could hear something in the trench coming from the direction they had been. "Can you hear that, Shadow?" he whispered.

They both looked along the trench, hoping it was not another Manflock. It wasn't. They couldn't believe what they saw: Hundreds and hundreds of rats were running toward them, some of them almost running along the sidewall, crammed so tightly, trying to overtake each other. "Oh, my word, we're dead!" stated Rambo.

"No. Stay still. They are trying to avoid the smoke; that's all."

"Oh, I hope you're right," Rambo responded, eyes tightly shut and holding his breath. The rats ploughed into them, some still bloody from their feast, bumping, jumping, and squealing as they went. Sure enough, as Shadow had said, they soon passed and headed toward the Manflock ahead of them.

"I wonder what he will make of that?" Shadow said, smiling. The man looked toward this flood of rats heading unceasingly toward him. "What the...? Oh, crap!" And in an instant, he was gone. His legs acted like springs, launching him high into the smokey blanket. They never saw him land. The rats continued on their way. The Manflock must have fallen into a neighbouring trench, as they could hear him mumbling to himself.

Shadow turned to his friend. "Well, that's handy. We can move forward now." Slightly shaken, but grateful to the rats, they continued toward the tree line; they hoped! Hours passed. "This is crazy. We will never find our way out of here. I need to rest." Shadow sat in the mud. Leaning against the side of the trench, he panted and shuffled his front legs forward, resting his head on them.

Rambo looked worryingly at his friend. "Rest there, my friend. I will look just a little farther. Don't worry; I won't go far." Rambo continued another hundred metres or so until the trench split into two. He wondered for a moment and decided the risk was too great. If he took a wrong turn, his friend would surely die in this terrible place. As he turned to go back, he realised that the smoke was at last leaving the ground. There seemed to be a gap between the ground and the ceiling of grey. He raised his head and realised he was just a few metres from a small barn. "Oh, I wonder, I wonder." He contemplated how he could get his friend just this short distance to where he could rest in comfort. He eagerly returned to Shadow, still lying in a pool of muddy water. "Shadow, Shadow, just a few more metres. Please, I promise you can rest then. Please!"

Shadow raised his head. "I can't get up! Give me a push, will you?"

Rambo lowered his head and gently pushed and lifted his friend from the mud. He was startled to discover how light Shadow was.

His ribs were clearly visible, and his thin legs were shaking. "Come, my friend, we can rest ahead."

Rambo stayed behind his friend. "Just a little farther, look, just there."

Shadow raised his head to see the side of a small barn. With a gentle push, Rambo lifted Shadow from the watery trench. "Come, my friend, we're nearly there." Rambo went forward and pushed the partly open door wide enough for them to get inside.

Once inside, both fell exhausted onto a thin layer of hay at the side of the barn. Apart from this bedding, it was empty but for a sack of some sort sitting in the corner near the door. Rambo thought he would examine the bag. He needed to find some food for Shadow, who was so weak. As he looked in the bag, he could see rubbish, but in amongst the paper and tins, there were bits of thrown-away food scraps, not much, but better than nothing. He sifted through the whole bag. There were bits of crust, a broken jar of honey about half full, two biscuits, and a big piece of smelly cheese. He looked at his friend. With coaxing, he managed to give Shadow the honey. Shadow was not strong enough to take anything else. Rambo then fell asleep.

When Rambo awoke, he looked to where Shadow had been lying. He was gone! Quickly, he sat up, calling, *"Shadow, Shadow!"*

"Here. I'm over here." Shadow was sitting by the door, looking out over the sight they had witnessed during the night. "What happed last night? How did we get here? And where did you get that food?"

Rambo looked at his friend and smiled. "Feeling a bit better?" he said.

"Better than most I've seen lately."

"Can't argue with that! Listen, we have to get back to the cave to meet with Sticky."

They made their way out of the little barn. It was not yet light, but they knew that dangers could be waiting for them outside. The smoke had moved. It was now clear enough for them to see the rocky outcrop in the distance where they had met Sticky. They decided to stay out of the muddy ditches, frightened they might get lost in the labyrinth of tracks. Instead, they decided to follow the woodland edge, and before long, they were safe in the little cave. Sticky had returned and was sleeping safely in the small crevice in the rock above them, so they decided to rest for a while, eagerly waiting for her to wake.

Today, they will be taken to meet Phoenix!

Chapter 14
Phoenix and Hope

Dusk arrived with heavy clouds and the promise of rain, but nothing could undo the excitement churning in their stomachs; there was no room for hunger this day! They sat side by side, silently looking up into the roof of the cave, patiently awaiting their friend Sticky. After what seemed like an age, yet was probably only a few moments, Sticky appeared. "Well, you two look keen."

The two looked at one another. "Sorry, Sticky, but we have come a long way for this day. We need to see Phoenix." Without a word, Sticky was airborne, swishing back and forth and calling, "Come on then, let's go. Not far, I promise."

They trekked over several fields, until in the distance, they could see a farm. The area looked well lighted, and from where they stood, they couldn't see many shadows in which they could conceal themselves.

They continued following Sticky toward the farm. In the night sky, grey smoke from the pyre rolled high into the distance, taking the foul smell of burning bodies with it.

As they got close to the barn, Sticky flew down to them, clinging to the bark of a tree. "Forgot to tell you; I sent a message up north for you. Have to wait for a while for news back, though."

"Thank you, Sticky, we're grateful for your help."

Sticky smiled. "You're welcome. Hope it helps. See that barn? Phoenix is in there."

The two looked at the barn. *What now?* they thought. "What do we do now?"

"Well, go on!" said Sticky. "I have told her you are coming." Gingerly, they moved forward. "If you go behind the barn, you will see a door. It's open!"

They peered into the barn but could see nothing. "Don't be afraid. Come on in; I am looking forward to meeting you."

They froze! The voice seemed so powerful. As they moved forward, the inside of the barn came into view. The upper slats of the side of the barn had light pouring through it from the brightly lit yard outside.

"Hello."

What they saw left them speechless. Standing before them was a glowing light. When she moved, dark shadows gave way to strong shafts of intense light. "Phoenix," they both said.

"Yes, my name is Phoenix. Please come and sit next to me. My friend, Sticky, has told me of your journey. I hope you won't be disappointed! She also told me that you, Shadow, are not too well. I have acquired food for you, lots of food, and for you, Rambo, lots of hay in the corner there."

They were mesmerised by this glowing spectacle. "Oh, thank you, oh, great Phoenix."

"I am no great anything, not at all. Look!" As she moved forward and out of the sharp rays of light, they saw her. Why, she was beautiful. She was pure white, but so young, even younger than Rambo. For a fleeting moment, it crossed their minds that they may have made a mistake. What could this young heifer do to help stop this killing? With authority, Phoenix stood forward. "Don't despair, my brave friends; I have much to tell you and good news. First, you must eat. If the door should open, I have prepared a place for you to hide behind the bales of hay there. You are safe here; your trials are over."

As Shadow tasted his first meal for many days, he looked at Phoenix. Phoenix told them how she was marched out into that very yard with her mother and the whole herd with her entire family. She was not long born and stayed close to her mother. Bang, bang, bang. One by one, the adults of the herd including her mother and finally her father the bull dropped to the ground. She told how a Manflock then pithed them all. Rambo and Shadow didn't need an explanation; they had seen it for themselves. "I was trapped beneath my dead mother. I continued to feed from her for two days, hoping she was just sleeping, until finally I knew she would not awake, as she was dead."

Shadow had stopped eating! "Oh, Phoenix, we're so sorry."

Phoenix continued, "Five days I was there until I heard a loud noise. As the Menflock scooped up the swollen bodies of my family, I heard one of them shout, 'Hey, there's a live one here!' In an instant, I was dragged out of there by my leg. Everything stopped while the Menflock discussed what to do with me. Some wished to kill me; others, that is, the Manflock here on the farm insisted that I should be allowed to live. I have been in here ever since!"

Although Phoenix didn't know it, her discovery had started a chain of events that was to change the Manflock approach to this foot and mouth outbreak and help finally to put an end to the killing of so many thousands of innocent animals. Indeed, she was the great Phoenix, but it was not over yet. Rambo was exhausted, but they were safe and warm with a warm bed too.

Two days passed. Phoenix and Rambo were getting worried about Shadow. He had not awakened since his meal two days earlier. "He's still breathing," said Rambo.

"He will wake soon. He was very weak when you both got here." Said Phoenix.

Shouting could be heard in the yard outside. "Oh, dear," said

Phoenix, "I wonder what that could mean." It didn't sound like angry voices, but it was very loud. A young female Manflock who lived at the farm burst into the barn. Rambo was so startled that he just stood in full view as she entered. Excited, she yelled, "You did it, Phoenix; you did it, girl. You are safe, and you have saved thousands of animals. You did it!"

She ran in circles in the barn not even noticing Rambo standing next to Phoenix. Bang! The barn door slammed. A few meters from the barn, she stopped. Scratching her head, she turned and, going back to the barn, opened the door. Looking toward Phoenix, she looked very confused. "I could have sworn … Did I see … Naah! I must be seeing things." And once more, the door was shut tight. As she walked away, she called back, "Well done, Phoenix, well done."

The commotion had finally woken Shadow, and they explained to him what had just occurred.

"Oh, Shadow, we may be able to go home soon." They looked at one another. Home was so far away. Was their family still alive?

Days passed, and Shadow was getting stronger. Apart from a daily visit from the young female to check on Phoenix, they had no threats to worry them. On the morning of the eighth day, two big bolts were slid back on the barn door. "Come on, girl." A Manflock appeared in the doorway. "Come on, girl, it's all over. You can come out now; come on out! Out!"

Phoenix walked gingerly toward the open door. The sun shone strongly this day. It was dry, warm, and welcoming. Rambo looked at Shadow. They both smiled. "We're going home!" Shadow said. They exploded out of the door and across the yard.

"*What the …*" cried the man. Startled, he jumped backward, falling into a newly filled drinking trough meant for Phoenix. The female who had thought she had seen a black ram but was not sure came running outside. Laughing, she shouted, "Mum, come look at this. Dad is having a bath." They all stood laughing at the wet farmer. Phoenix looked toward her friends. They stopped running and turned around. Shadow barked, and the Manflock family turned to see Shadow and Rambo looking back toward Phoenix. "Good-bye, our true friend, good-bye, oh, great Phoenix." They sat for a few seconds then turned and ran into the fields.

The family at the farm didn't know what this was all about. They turned to Phoenix, then looking at one another, they burst out laughing and went indoors. "That water was cold." His family laughed as the farmhouse door was closed. Phoenix was now alone in the yard. Finally, she looked up at the fields, but her friends had gone!

"Take care, my friends." She turned and took a drink from the slightly contaminated water butt (no pun intended).

Shadow and Rambo travelled as fast as they could, re-tracing their path. Still wary of the Menflock, they hoped to get to the farm where Willow lived. They knew that if the sheep there were to be moved back to their farm in the north, they would be able to get a ride as they did before. Days passed and, although Shadow was a lot stronger, he was still far from his normal self. It took all his energy to keep up with Rambo. Rambo stopped. Shadow was close behind and, with his head low, walked into him. "Sorry," Rambo smiled, "Look!" There it was, the very farm. Filled with hope, they looked over the fields but could see no sheep. "Oh, Shadow, have we have missed them, or have they been killed?"

"Please, Rambo, we can't think like that. Let's go and find out."

Together, they ventured toward the gate. They thought it best to go around the yard and into the barn. If the sheep were not at the farm, then Willow would not be either, and they would not be able to get home. They would surely die here.

They looked into the barn through a small hole left in a board when a knot became loose and fell out. Shadow's collar still hung high up on the beam in the roof space. Willow couldn't be seen. That familiar knot in the stomach was back! Through a small opening, they entered the barn. The old tractor was there, and the discarded tire they'd hid in was still lying on the floor. There were fewer bales of hay, but there was still enough to hide them.

Not sure what to do, they climbed up onto the bales of hay and settled down. "I don't know what to do," said Rambo.

Shadow looked at his friend, thinking, *Is this where we finish our journey?* Thoughts of home again filled their minds.

Click! The door, that squeaky wicket gate, opened. In walked the farmer. It was him! It was the farmer from the farm in the north. "Willow, come here, girl."

They leapt into the air. "Oh, could it be, could it really be her?"

Slowly, Willow walked across the yard from the farmhouse. Shadow and Rambo looked at one another. "Is she okay?" asked Rambo. As she came into the barn, the farmer gave her a cup of sweet tea and a bowl of food. After patting her on the head, he left her alone, or so he thought. Shadow slowly came down from the hay bales.

On hearing the rustling behind her, she tuned to see a filthy, half-starved, red-eyed, shaking Shadow. "Oh, Shadow! My poor friend, what you must have been through."

Shadow sat, ears down and looking so weak. "Are you okay, Willow?"

"I am fine. Tell you all about it later." Using her wet, shiny nose, she nudged the bowl of sweet tea and food toward Shadow. After just a couple of attempts at eating, Shadow fell to one side in the scattered hay.

"Shadow!" called Rambo, "Shadow, are you okay?" Shadow was lying motionless.

Willow settled at his side, licking his wounds. There were so many that she couldn't count them. "Rambo, come down here; it's so good to see you both. We have to move Shadow. The farmer will be back soon!"

No sooner had she finished speaking than the familiar squeal of the gate allowed the farmer access to the barn. On seeing Shadow, he ran from the barn.

"I know where he has gone! We have to move him quick!" insisted Willow. Sure enough, the farmer had gone to get his brother's shotgun. He intended to finish the job. On his return, the door got his head again. "Damn and blast that door. I hate that door. Joe!" he yelled.

He stood tall and slid two cartridges into the weapon. Willow was barking and standing in front of Shadow. "Okay, girl, I'll get him." The farmer stopped for a moment. Lowering his gun, he said, "Hang on a mo. Just how the hell did you get here?" He recognised the dog as the same one he had taken a shot at on his farm at home. "That's not possible, is it?"

Willow sat in front of Shadow, protecting him from the farmer. "Oh, if only you ever wanted to understand what I say, understand this!" She was barking frantically, running at the farmer then back to Shadow until she lay across him, whimpering.

The farmer, realising he had no need to rush due to the impoverished condition of the poor dog, put his weapon safely down and placed his hands on his hips. *I've seen enough killin'*, he thought. With a deep sigh, he walked toward the two dogs. Willow lowered her head and growled, showing all her teeth.

"Okay, girl, don't worry; I won't hurt him." Willow stepped aside.

"Oh, my goodness, what a state you are in." He turned to call his brother. As he turned, he noticed Rambo. Flinching, he shook his head. "Just what the hell is this, Noah's ark? Derek, Derek, come here, quick!"

Together, they stood, confused by the strange events. "Well," said Bob, "That is a Welsh Mountain Black, though what it's doing here can only be imagined." He was right; no one could imagine the journey these two fearless friends had undertaken. "Well, not much hope for this dog, don't think. We'll see."

On saying that, Derek picked up Shadow and walked toward the farmhouse. Bob turned to Rambo, "Well, as you are a bit displaced. You better come with me up north where ya should be."

Rambo was held tightly and led toward the familiar trailer. "In you go, ram." The door closed behind him.

"Hey, look who it is!" His old friends were alive!

"Oh, it's so good to see you all." He answered questions all day long until he asked them, "When will we be moving? When is the farmer taking us north? I can't leave this place without Shadow."

"Well, we have been in here all day, so soon, we hope."

Rambo was so pleased that Shadow was being looked after but unsure what was to do next.

That evening, the two brothers discussed the future of the two strays. "Well, if you have no objection, I would take both the dog and ram back up north with me. I will need another dog until Willow is up to working again."

"No problem Bob," said Derek, "and yes, you are right about the ram; it needs to be on the hills."

Shadow lay sleeping under the kitchen table. "He be ready to move tomorrow. I know he will need time, but I think he be okay. Vet said he be fine, just need feeding up, is all," said Joe. "Mind if I stay another night, Derek? I be on me way tomorrow."

"I'll put the kettle on," he said, grinning. They pushed some fresh hey into the trailer for the sheep and went indoors.

The following day, Shadow was awake. No sign of Willow or Rambo, so he was a little worried. Still in the farmhouse he was not sure what was happening.

"Well, that was a damn fine breakfast, damn fine. I'll be on me way. Dog seems okay, so I'll put him in the barn till I sort Willow out."

Without further ado, Shadow was taken to the barn. He wondered where his friends where and tried to see across the yard. Still too weak to climb high, he waited and listened to all the commotion outside.

"Okay, all sorted!"

Shadow was taken to the trailer and put inside. He looked around and smiled, glad to be amongst friends again. "Rambo." They both smiled. As Shadow turned, he saw Willow lying in a hay-filled bed at the front of the trailer. He looked at her and went numb all over. "Oh Willow, Willow I have missed you so much". Looking into the straw bed Shadow became lost for words, Erm, hello, erm, are they ... erm, are they ... erm, my erm ..."

Willow looked wonderful. They had been concerned she was not too well. Willow looked at Shadow, "Yes, Shadow. Come and say hello to your family."

Feeding at her breast were seven, no, eight, newborn puppies. Shadow fell quiet. "Oh, my Willow." He belly-crawled over to them, sniffing his new family. He spent the whole journey licking Willow, only stopping to look at his eight puppies. He didn't notice the swishing sound as they crossed the great waters. He didn't even notice the bumpy lane back at the farm. In fact, he was unaware of anything else until there was a sharp bang! It told him the trailer was about to be opened.

"Home, sheep and stowaways." Said the farmer.

The farmer's wife came running out of the farmhouse. "Where are my new puppies then?" she asked.

"Inside, my dear, all safe and sound. Got an extra one in there for you; needs a bit TLC, I think."

"Oh, my poor dear." This reception was different to the one they received on their previous visit. Once they were all out of the trailer, the dogs were put together into the barn, and the sheep, along with Rambo, were put into the field to enjoy some fresh grass.

Oh, that's so good, thought Rambo, and dreams of going home seemed realistic at last.

Days later, Shadow and Willow walked together across the yard.

As they came to the gate, they stopped. *Click, click, click.* Rambo smiled and turned around. "That sound can mean only one thing. Shadow! How are you feeling?" They stood at the gate, talking.

"Hey, missus, come look at this." The farmer's wife drew back the curtain, and they stood watching this little huddle for a few moments. "Something going on with that lot, something strange, I recon."

His wife turned to him saying, "Only you could think that. Only you could think they are up to something. I sure you think you are Doctor Doolittle."

Meanwhile, Shadow was telling Rambo that he would not be going back to home hill and was going to stay on the farm. He had a family to care for.

Rambo told him he was going to miss his friend and said goodbye to them both. "I will be leaving tonight. I will ask Pippa to let you know if all is okay, but you must not follow your place is here." Rambo was hoping to get to the woodland they had left so very long ago. Willow and Shadow stood side by side and watched Rambo disappear over the fields.

Shadow felt a little worried for Rambo, not knowing what he may or indeed may not find on Home Hill. He discussed this fear with Willow, and they both agreed that, if they didn't hear from Pippa in the next seven days, he would follow Rambo. Shadow was still very weak and would be of no use to Rambo. He would, indeed, slow him down.

Rambo made good progress. He was, of course, worried that his family was gone but was driven forward by the hope of seeing them all again. As he continued along the woodland track, he recognised the point at which they had previously dropped down into the forest. He turned into the woodland. "Now, if I could only remember how to get to the barn. Pippa did explain it, but it was so long ago." He thought deeply about his problem. A bush moved nearby. "Who's that? Come out now!" he demanded. "*Hailwen!* I thought you had been taken."

"I was taken," she replied. "I was exploring the woodland. There were strange noises and smells. I had to have a look."

"Is that when the woodland creatures captured you?"

"Woodland creatures? *No!* Not woodland creatures. I was just looking to see over a small ridge and was grabbed by a young female Manflock. I've never seen one so small. She took me to a Manflock, and they locked me in a small barn; hiding me, they said! I was in there for ages, anyway, for some reason, they unlocked the barn , and I fled back here only to find you had all gone. I've been here two days now!"

Rambo looked at her. "You have grown a lot!"

"You too!"

The two talked a little while until they decided to go deep into the forest to located Pippa's barn. They hoped that Tom, Gwen, Slight, and little Bethan would still be there, safe and well. Neither of them knew that Slight had left the little band to return to the hill. Hours passed. "All these trees look the same."

"Yes, they do, but it can't be far now," replied Rambo. Stopping, he said, "Look! Is that it?" Through a gap in the trees, there stood a most impressive barn.

"Bit big for a bat," said Hailwen.

"I didn't mean she built it!" replied Rambo.

Together, they walked toward the barn, yes, right across the open meadow that lay before it. After a distance of maybe a hundred metres, they stopped.

"It's very quiet," said Hailwen. As they walked on, they were very apprehensive about what lay ahead.

Inside the barn were Tom, Gwen, and not-so-little Bethan. Tom was looking out of the barn through a small hole, big enough for one eye to peer through. He looked, stepped back, then stepped forward, and looked again. "Gwen, I need you here." His voice was shaking.

"What is it?" Thinking the worst, she ran to his side.

"Look!" She peered through the small hole and let out a mighty yell, *"Hailwen, Rambo!"* She quickly ran out of the barn and stood looking at her lost ones. Bethan and Tom soon followed. All looked for a few moments. After tears of joy, they returned as a reunited family into the barn and talked of their adventures until late into the night. Rambo told the good news of Shadow and his new family, "I am sure he will visit us during the summer." Pippa joined in the celebrations and was only too pleased to carry the news of the family being reunited, "Wow, this is great. I will go tonight, yes, this very night. I've got good news to tell, and I will let them all know they are welcome to visit soon." That evening Pippa left early, swishing to and fro, excited and happy once more.

The following day, they made their way along the tracks, leaving the protection of the woodland behind them. They passed the pile of stones and continued toward Home Hill.

As they approached, they stopped and looked into the muddy hole in which they had hidden so long ago. As the sun rose, they stood high on the hill, and as the light grew brighter, no red patches could be seen. There were not many sheep on the hills, but they were not alone either!

Epilogue

AFTER listening to this long tale, the little ram looked at his father. "Father, did you know these sheep?"

"Yes, my little one. Look. See over there? That's your mother."

"Yes, I know that, Father."

"Her name is Hailwen."

The little ram looked on in awe at her brave mother.

His father said, "Look over there. See your grandparents? Their names are Tom and Gwen. And if you look far over on the next hill, you can see a little family of sheep. My sister Bethan now has a family of her own."

"But, Father, if ... and they ... then you must be ..."

"Yes, my little ram, I am *Rambo!*"

As the little ram looked up at Rambo, two birds flew overhead. "Aaaaaachoooo, oh dear, I don't feel too good. I think I am getting the flu."

Oh, dear! Here we go again.

Lightning Source UK Ltd.
Milton Keynes UK
171224UK00001B/51/P